Speaking of not knowing what hit you…

CiCi did a double take when she saw the man in the doorway. She'd checked out his picture in the team program but the camera didn't do him justice.

Jake Culpepper wasn't classically handsome, but with dark hair that was long enough to curl around his collar, pale green eyes and eyelashes a mile long, he oozed sex appeal.

He was obviously the epitome of everything CiCi hated, an arrogant jock with an ego the size of Dallas.

So why was she staring at him like a smitten schoolgirl?

Dear Reader,

Hill Country Hero is a "chuckle" kind of book and, considering its origin, that's not surprising. A couple of years back there was a PR gimmick at a baseball game that featured a race between some ballpark food mascots—a hot dog, a wurst, etc. One of the baseball players decided it would be funny to deck the hotdog. That was obviously a case of more brawn than brain. But it was a great inspiration for the start of this book.

The question is—can a professional football player from the wrong side of the tracks and an heiress to a Texas-sized auto empire find true love despite their differences? Absolutely! Cupid might be sporting a cowboy hat but his aim's pretty darned accurate.

I love hearing from my readers. You can contact me at adefee@earthlink.net.

I hope you enjoy your trip to the Texas Hill Country—one of my favorite places.

Ann

Hill Country Hero
Ann DeFee

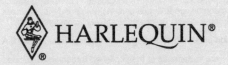

HARLEQUIN®

TORONTO • NEW YORK • LONDON
AMSTERDAM • PARIS • SYDNEY • HAMBURG
STOCKHOLM • ATHENS • TOKYO • MILAN • MADRID
PRAGUE • WARSAW • BUDAPEST • AUCKLAND

Book acknowledgments are generally made to people,
but I've decided to stretch the imagination
and dedicate this story to that magical place
called the Texas Hill Country where the rivers run
clear and cold, the people are the salt of the earth
and the cobalt skies stretch to eternity.

Recycling programs
for this product may
not exist in your area.

ISBN-13: 978-0-373-75300-0

HILL COUNTRY HERO

Copyright © 2010 by Ann DeFee.

www.eHarlequin.com

Printed in U.S.A.

ABOUT THE AUTHOR

Ann DeFee's debut novel, *A Texas State of Mind* (Harlequin American Romance), was a double finalist in the 2006 Romance Writers of America's prestigious RITA® Awards.

Drawing on her background as a fifth-generation Texan, Ann loves to take her readers into the sassy and sometimes wacky world of a small Southern community. As an air force wife with twenty-three moves under her belt, she's now settled in her tree house in the Pacific Northwest with her husband, their golden retriever and two very spoiled cats. When she's not writing, you can probably find her on the tennis court or in the park with her walking group.

Books by Ann DeFee

HARLEQUIN AMERICAN ROMANCE

HARLEQUIN EVERLASTING LOVE

Don't miss any of our special offers. Write to us at the following address for information on our newest releases.

Harlequin Reader Service
U.S.: 3010 Walden Ave., P.O. Box 1325, Buffalo, NY 14269
Canadian: P.O. Box 609, Fort Erie, Ont. L2A 5X3

TEXAS HILL COUNTRY PEACH CRISP

3 cups sliced fresh peaches
¼ cup butter, softened
1¼ cups sugar, divided
1 cup flour
1 tsp baking powder
½ tsp salt
½ cup milk
1 tbsp cornstarch
¼ tsp ground nutmeg
1 cup boiling water
Whipping cream or ice cream

Place peach slices in an 8-inch square baking pan. Cream butter and ¾ cup sugar. Combine flour, baking powder and salt; add to creamed mixture alternately with milk. Spoon mixture over fruit. Sift together remaining ½ cup sugar, cornstarch and nutmeg; sprinkle over batter. Pour boiling water over top. Bake at 350 degrees for 1 hour. Serve with whipping cream or ice cream.

Chapter One

It was official. Collier Channing "CiCi" Hurst (formerly Tank-ersley) was slowly but surely losing her mind. And what was her first clue? Could it be that she was seriously thinking about asking Daddy for a job?

CiCi had had a *bad* year and a half starting with finding her scum-sucking, low-life ex-husband studying the *Kama Sutra* with Marian the Librarian. Did William "Tank" Tankersley even *know* how to read?

CiCi gazed at the frilly pink canopy above her head. She was thirty-two years old and sleeping in her teenage bedroom under a faded Pearl Jam poster. It had been almost a year since she'd signed the final divorce decree and she was still rudderless.

Talk about pitiful!

There were so many things she could blame Tank for. He didn't want children, so CiCi put her dream of a big family on the back burner. Tank didn't want her to work outside the home, so her Stanford degree in adolescent psychology went unused. Tank didn't want—

Stop it!

The doormat phase of her life was over. It was time to move on.

Fortunately money wasn't a problem. Tank was a Pro Bowl right tackle for the National Football League's Green Bay

Packers, and as a result of his lucrative contracts and a wise investment counselor, he was set for life. And since they were divorced in Wisconsin, which was a community property state, CiCi was financially secure, too.

But Tank's adultery and the subsequent divorce had taken a machete to CiCi's self-esteem, and that was probably why she was so indecisive. Meaningful jobs in her field generally required an advanced degree but she wasn't ready to delve into a master's program.

Back to the problem at hand—despite a college degree and six years of volunteer work, the only serious employment CiCi had been able to find was as a substitute teacher. Considering the way some kids tested subs, that wasn't her dream job. And now that summer had arrived, even that opportunity had gone by the wayside.

Her divorced high school buddies had rebounded by snagging new husbands, always richer than the original. CiCi, on the other hand, wasn't about to risk tying the knot with another loser like Tank.

Just the thought of dating or having anything to do with the opposite sex was enough to give her a raging headache, so CiCi mentally segued to an easier problem—finding a place of her own. Retreating to Mama and Daddy's had given her a chance to regroup, but she couldn't stay there forever. The question was should she rent, buy or pitch a tent in the Galleria parking lot. Scratch that last one. Houston summers were as hot as the tropics on steroids.

This whole situation was making her crazy. It was day three hundred and forty of her self-imposed exile and it was time for a change. On that note, CiCi rolled out of bed and headed to the kitchen for breakfast. If she was really going to hit Daddy up for employment, it was now or never. What did she have to lose besides her pride…and dignity…and—

"Good morning, sleepyhead." Marianne Hurst, aka Mama,

was at the stove, making breakfast. She was petite, blonde and beautiful. CiCi's sisters—Mackenzie and Minerva (Mac and Mia)—were carbon copies of their mother, whereas CiCi was tall with olive skin and dark hair. Mama claimed she must have come from a long-lost Gypsy bloodline.

"It's only six-thirty." CiCi plopped down at the long trestle table that had seen many Hurst family meals. "Is Daddy still here or has he already left for work?"

"Whatcha need, baby doll?" CiCi hadn't noticed her father rummaging in the industrial-size Sub-Zero refrigerator. Daddy was a business mogul with a Harvard education, but he also had the ability to magically morph into Texas Bob Hurst, owner of half the Cadillac/Hummer/GMC dealerships in the Lone Star State.

"Well, uh."

"Spit it out, kiddo," Daddy said, pulling a pitcher of orange juice from the fridge. "Would you like some?" He held up the carafe.

"Sure." CiCi handed him her glass. "I was, uh, I was thinking that maybe you might have a job for me at one of your dealerships." There, she'd done it and the sun was still shining.

"Oh, dear," Mama muttered, exchanging a glance with her husband. They'd been married so long they were able to communicate without words.

Winston "Texas Bob" Hurst chomped into his piece of toast. He paused, chewed some more, then shook his head. "The dealerships aren't hiring right now—we've been lucky not to lay anyone off. But let me think." Texas Bob took one bite and then another.

Things weren't looking good.

"What about doing something with the Road Runners?"

"The Road Runners?" Was he kidding? Daddy's National Football League team was the last place she wanted to work.

He might not have noticed, but CiCi hated jocks. Abhorred, detested, loathed and despised— Oh, never mind.

"I don't think so."

"Seriously, everyone else in the family is involved in the organization. Your mother oversees our charitable work. Mia's doing a great job as our director of public relations and Mac's having a ball working with the Road Runner cheerleaders."

"What do you suggest?"

Before Texas Bob could respond, a tiny blond dynamo dressed in Bratz pajamas whirled in, followed by her equally perky mom. CiCi wasn't the only sister who had retreated to the sanctuary of the family home. When Mackenzie and her quarterback husband split, she'd also made the move back to Houston.

"Mac, what do you think?" Mama asked. Darn it, she was double-teaming.

"About what?" CiCi's sister asked. A veteran multi-tasker, she was simultaneously filling her coffee mug, picking up her six-year-old daughter, Molly, and making toast.

"We're trying to talk CiCi into working for the Road Runners," Daddy answered.

Mac squealed but then she must have had second thoughts. "Uh, doing what?"

"That's what I'd like to know," CiCi grumbled.

"Could she help you with the cheerleaders?" Mama asked.

"Well, hmm." Mac looked as if she was working on a complicated mathematical equation.

"Don't stress yourself," CiCi snapped. God, she hated sounding so testy.

Mac blew her a raspberry. "Do you know how to dance?"

"Of course not." It was a standing joke that CiCi was the only Hurst to ever drop out of ballet class.

"Perhaps she could work in the accounting department," Mac suggested.

That one really got a chuckle. Math was not CiCi's strong suit—in fact, she wasn't sure she'd even been dealt a hand.

"Tell you what, baby doll," Daddy said. "Why don't you come down to the football minicamp this afternoon? We'll see what we can find."

CICI HATED TO ADMIT IT but she was fascinated by the energy and glamour of the Road Runners. She didn't want anything to do with football players, but she could still admire the way they filled out their uniforms. Just because they were off-limits to her didn't mean she couldn't look.

The Road Runner cheerleaders were also beautiful, sexy and well endowed. Add it all together and it was quite a heady environment.

CiCi stood in the tunnel leading to the locker rooms. Although there wasn't an audience, there was the residual energy left by 65,000 screaming fans. The skill positions— the quarterbacks, the wide receivers and the tight ends—were practicing the expertise that made the game so thrilling, and the cheerleaders were going through their first full day of rehearsal. All in all, it was an exciting place.

CiCi strolled across the artificial turf, watching as the athletes warmed up. These guys weren't the three-hundred-plus-pound behemoths who'd play on the defensive line, but they were fine specimens. Bulging biceps, muscled legs, broad chests— Whoa! Stop right there. CiCi had sworn off men. That was her story and she was sticking to it.

"Hey, sis!" Mac yelled. It was the only way she could be heard over the noise from the field. "Come here."

Mac was wearing a pair of low-slung shorts, a midriff top and a ponytail. She was in her midthirties but could easily pass for a teenager.

"I've got it," she squealed when CiCi strolled over. "I know the perfect job for you."

Sometimes Mac could be such a blonde, CiCi thought.

"What?"

"You can be the chicken." She clapped her hands in glee. Her enthusiasm was almost catching. Almost.

"The chicken? Do you mean that thing?" CiCi pointed at Tex, the team mascot, who was standing on the sidelines watching the cheerleaders. The costume was supposed to be a road runner—otherwise known as a prairie chicken—but swear to goodness, it was a dead ringer for Foghorn Leghorn from the cartoons.

"Why would I want to do that? And what about the guy who's wearing it?"

"It's not a problem. Dwayne Scruggs has been trying to find someone to take over for him. I think he's in trouble with his probation officer and he wants to beat feet. He has a record, you know." Mac whispered the last sentence, not that Dwayne could hear her.

"Daddy hired an ex-con?" That was astonishing.

"I think he's only done county jail time. He got the job because he's Jake Culpepper's cousin."

"Who's Jake Culpepper?"

"Oh, sweetie, you are so out of the loop. Jake's our star tight end." Mac fanned herself. "And, man, are his buns tight."

"Mackenzie!"

As usual, her sister ignored her. "Hey, Dwayne! Get yourself over here," she shouted.

CiCi grabbed her arm. "Wait! I don't know if I want to do this."

"Sure you do. This is exactly what you need." Mac was so proud of herself she was almost dancing in place.

Tex nodded his head and waddled over.

"Dwayne, my sister wants to take over the chicken gig."

"I don't—" CiCi started to object but didn't get very far.

"No foolin'? Babes, it's all yours." Dwayne shucked out of the chicken suit so fast it looked as if he had a load of hot briquettes in his britches.

"Here." He tossed her a two-foot chicken head with a crest of glossy feathers that Sally Rand would have envied. "They're practicing the sideline show now." He waved toward the field at the bevy of buxom dancers in short skirts and tight midriff tops. "Check with the head honcho and see what she wants you to do." Following that suggestion, the former chicken raced off.

"What was that all about?" CiCi asked.

"Beats me. He's nuts." Then Mackenzie broke into a big smile. "But think of it this way. You have a job."

Yep, she did. However, jumping into a giant feathered costume in the middle of a Houston summer was almost as appealing as snorting Jell-O. It would be hot, sticky work—and bad hair was inevitable, but sometimes a girl had to gut up. If she could make this chicken shtick work, she'd be a part of the team *and* she'd have a job. All things considered, any position was better than unemployment.

The only thing that kept CiCi from breaking into a happy dance was her pesky inner voice that sounded like a rerun of *Lost in Space.*

Warning! Warning! Warning!

Her last experience with an athlete had ended in disaster, Would this be any different? Oh, boy, it sure better be.

CiCi glanced at the chicken head (okay, it was a road runner) and then studied the rest of the suit. She could flap her feathers with the best of them. The feet might be a bit tricky, but the wings would be a piece of cake. Now, if she could shut up that niggle of doubt, everything would be fine.

Chapter Two

Jake Culpepper was going to freakin' throttle his lily-livered, dirtbag cousin Dwayne. That jerk had committed grand theft auto and was the reason Jake's prize Porsche was in auto intensive care. Thanks to him, Jake was reduced to driving a rusty, manure-covered pickup. It was the only vehicle available at his ranch that morning.

There was no need to get his blood pressure up—it was just a car, not the end of the world. Yeah, and comparing his sleek beauty to a common vehicle was like comparing the F-22 Raptor to the Wright Brothers' Kitty Hawk.

To add insult to injury, after Dwayne hit a telephone pole in the "borrowed" car, he'd abandoned it on the highway. But since the dweeb was already on probation, calling the cops on him wasn't an option.

And Dwayne was only the tip of the bad-news iceberg. On the family front, Jake's mom had hooked up with another loser. He loved her like crazy, but her taste in men sucked. Every time she got involved with a new guy, it cost Jake an enormous amount of time, money and heartburn.

The "biggie" was that Jake's contract was up for renewal. If the Road Runners didn't sign him, he'd become a free agent, and that would mean a move. And considering the trouble his relatives regularly indulged in, Jake really didn't want to leave

Texas. He'd spent most of his life taking care of his family, and that was a hard habit to break.

In most professions a guy was just getting started at thirty. Not so for athletes. Thirty was pushing it, and although Jake had a great agent—who worked hard to earn his fifteen percent—the contract situation was still unresolved.

But on the bright side, Jake had plenty of money in the bank and his social life was, to say the least, hot. He'd been voted Houston's most-eligible bachelor two years in a row.

And best of all, he'd bought the ranch of his dreams— hundreds of acres of coastal plains grazing land. Overall, life was sweet. As long as he could keep cousins Dwayne and Darrell out of trouble. He'd never be able to change his mother's taste in men, but he did what he could to provide her with everything she'd ever want or need.

Oh, well, exercise-induced endorphins were the best pick-me-up known to man, and the field was the only place Jake could butt heads without getting arrested.

If Dwayne was smart, he wouldn't show his face at the stadium for at least the next decade. But that dude wasn't Einstein. In fact, Big Bird was probably smarter than his cousin.

Jake pulled the filthy pickup into the parking lot, hesitating a moment before claiming his reserved parking spot. If his luck held, he could sneak in and then gripe about the gardener taking his space. The truck let out a giant belch of smoke when Jake cut the engine.

"Cool wheels." That comment came from Cole Benavides, the Road Runners' quarterback and Jake's best friend. Jake had been so busy trying to see through the smoke he hadn't noticed Cole pull into the adjacent spot.

Anonymity was impossible. "Up yours," Jake mumbled as he grabbed his duffel bag from the bed of the truck.

Cole acknowledged the wisecrack with a chuckle. "Good junior-high comeback."

In spite of himself, Jake grinned. "I'll show you junior high." He poked Cole in the ribs, initiating the ritual of goosing and grabbing they'd perfected during their four years at Texas A&M.

"Seriously, what happened to your wheels?"

"Dwayne happened." Jake explained the demise of his treasured Porsche.

"That bites. What are you going to do?"

"I can't turn him in to the cops, since he's still on probation, but if I catch him, I'm gonna pummel him within an inch of his life. His rear end isn't going to be worth a plug nickel."

Cole laughed. "Let's hope he doesn't show. I'd hate to have to spring for your bail. And speaking of butts, we'd better get moving or the coach is gonna have ours."

"CULPEPPER, get your rear on the field and get warmed up. This ain't no ladies' sewing circle." Those tender words came from Coach Carruthers, the toughest coach in the NFL.

Jake closed his cell phone. He'd been talking to AAA, making sure his car had been delivered to the dealer's repair shop. He wished he could call the cops, but even though Dwayne was in dire need of a comeuppance, Jake simply couldn't do it. Mama would have a conniption—and even tough guys didn't cross their moms.

"Sure, Coach, I'm outta here." Jake pulled the jersey over his shoulder pads and trotted out on the field. He'd barely made it to the twenty-yard line when he spied Dwayne on the sidelines clucking and flapping in his mascot costume as though he didn't have a care in the world. Boy, did that moron have another think coming.

"Hey, Culpepper, get over here." Jake heard Cole, but he

was too focused on the chicken to care. Ten yards, five yards, two yards—and a big fat splat!

Jake didn't plan to hurt the jerk. Dwayne was family, even if he was a doofus. It was just going to be a friendly tussle—no big deal. Too bad he hadn't counted on the ramifications of tackling a six-foot featherbed. Jake spit fluff out of his mouth and had to admit that this hadn't been one of his better ideas.

Cole pulled him up by his jersey and smacked him on the arm. "Culpepper, you are *such* an idiot. Do you know who that is?"

Of course he knew who it was. He wouldn't tackle just *anyone.* "Yeah, it's Dwayne." He reached down to give his cousin a hand up.

Cole shot him one of those grins that meant trouble with a capital *T.* "Like I said, you're such an idiot." He stepped in front of Jake and addressed the chicken. "Are you okay?"

"Hmmmph."

"Tell you what. Flap your wings if you need help getting the head off."

Feathers flew as the chicken wings pumped up and down accompanied by frenzied sound effects.

"Hmmmmph, hmmmph, hmmmph!"

Cole patted down the puffed feathers. "Give me a sec." He glanced at Jake. "Get over here, dumb ass, I have something to show you." He was still grinning widely. "Boy, are you in trouble!"

What was he talking about? There wasn't a soul who cared if he pounded Dwayne. In fact, the Road Runner gals would probably line up to give him high-fives.

Cole swept the mascot costume head off with a flourish. "What do you say to this?"

Jake gaped. "This" was a tall, slender woman with big

brown eyes, a pixie haircut and Cupid's bow lips. Jeeze, Louise. He'd decked some gorgeous chick.

He outweighed her by at least a hundred pounds. Damn! She could have been seriously hurt. Thank God for all those feathers!

First he'd had to deal with Dwayne's shenanigans and now he had a pissed-off Ashley Judd look-alike on his hands. Would someone please put him out of his misery?

The irate beauty whapped him upside the head with her wing. "You cretin!"

If looks could kill, he'd be pushing up daisies. That wasn't the reaction he generally got from women. A quick assessment convinced Jake that Miss I'd-Like-to-Snap-Your-Head-Off was okay.

"Oh, boy." Cole grimaced. "Don't look now, but here comes Texas Bob. I sure wouldn't want to be in your cleats."

Great, just what he needed. Texas Bob Hurst wasn't going to be happy about this latest screw-up, and with his contract renewal coming up, Jake did want to stay on the boss's good side.

Much to Jake's surprise, Texas Bob put his arms around as much of the chicken as he could hold.

"Is my baby girl okay?" He didn't wait for an answer before he turned his glare on Jake.

Baby girl! Baby girl, as in the man's daughter? Crap, his ass was definitely grass.

"You." Texas Bob stabbed a finger in Jake's direction. "My office—twenty minutes. No excuses."

Jake watched the chicken clomp off the field behind her father. He glanced at Cole. "That's bad, huh?"

His friend slapped him on the back. "Definitely."

Several of his teammates had crowded around to check out the action, and in unison, they shook their heads.

As they say in Texas—well, shee-it!

Chapter Three

Ten minutes later, CiCi had been examined by the team doctor. Thanks to the multiple layers of padding in the mascot costume, she'd escaped the hard tackle with only a couple of bruises.

"Daddy, I'm sure there's a perfectly reasonable explanation for what happened. Don't do something you'll regret," CiCi said as she looked through the office refrigerator. She was tempted by the chilled chardonnay but decided to grab a bottle of water.

Texas Bob leaned back in his large leather chair. "Don't worry, sweetheart. I knew I needed to cool down before I talked to him. That's why I gave him twenty minutes to get up here. Are you positive you're not hurt?" In the boardroom Winston Hurst was as tough as nails, but when it came to his family, he was a big marshmallow.

"I'm fine. Really." CiCi could swear on a stack of bibles and it wouldn't matter one whit. Daddy had made up his mind and nothing she said would change it.

So to keep her thoughts off whatever Daddy was planning, CiCi sat down to peruse the roster listing Jake Culpepper's stats. Holy tamale, the guy was six foot five and weighed two hundred and sixty pounds. No wonder she felt as if she'd been hit by a bus.

"I have a great idea. I think you'll like it." Daddy drummed his fingers on the desk. His face was creased in the shark grin that had struck fear in the hearts of men all over the state. Poor Jake Culpepper wasn't going to know what hit him.

And speaking of which, CiCi did a double take when she saw the man himself in the doorway. She'd checked out his picture in the team program but the camera didn't do him justice. And on the field, she'd been seeing stars.

Jake Culpepper wasn't classically handsome, but with dark hair that was just long enough to curl around his collar, pale green eyes and eyelashes a mile long, he oozed sex appeal.

He was obviously everything CiCi hated—an arrogant jock with an ego the size of Dallas. So why was she staring at him like a smitten schoolgirl?

"Sir," Jake said, addressing Texas Bob. Then he walked to the couch where CiCi was sitting with her feet curled up under her.

"Ms. Hurst, I can't tell you how sorry I am. Did I hurt you?"

CiCi shook her head. It wasn't often she was at a loss for words, but right now she couldn't do much more than gape. Fortunately, Jake didn't seem to notice that she'd turned into a zombie.

"I never would have pulled that stunt if I'd known you were in the chicken suit. I thought you were my cousin Dwayne. He stole my car this morning and wrecked it, so I thought I'd teach him a lesson. I wasn't planning anything major. I figured we'd just have a little scuffle." Somehow, during his explanation, he'd managed to get close enough to take her hand.

When CiCi realized what he was doing, she snatched it away. Charming jocks should be banned from society. They weren't trustworthy. Like her philandering ex. They'd pledged to love each other through good times and bad, but that promise had obviously meant nothing to Tank. So it was goodbye to her marriage and hello to a crisis of self-confidence.

"Looks like you really stepped in it this time, Culpepper." Texas Bob stacked his hands behind his head. "Sit. I have an offer I don't think you'll be able to refuse."

CiCi had a flashback to the *Godfather* movie. She glanced at Jake and discovered he was probably thinking the same thing. Nevertheless, he took a seat in one of the lush leather chairs.

"I was on my way out to the field to talk to my daughter when I saw you assault her." Daddy's face had turned an alarming shade of red. "I almost had a heart attack. What the hell were you thinking?" He slammed his hands on the massive walnut desk. "You could have killed her."

"Sir—"

"Did I say I wanted to hear from you?"

"Uh, no, sir." Jake slumped back in his chair.

She almost felt sorry for him. "It's okay, Daddy. *I'm* okay. No harm, no foul. I'm sure he—" she waved a hand in the athlete's direction "—didn't mean to hurt me. So let's just forget it."

Jake started to speak but Texas Bob cut him off. "Son, your contract's up this year." His smile didn't make it to his eyes. "And as team owner I make the final decision about exercising our option to sign you again."

Jake sighed. "Yes, sir. I realize that."

Texas Bob seemed satisfied by his answer, and turned back to his daughter. "I have a great idea. I got a call this morning from Camp Touchdown. The director we had lined up for the summer left without bothering to give me notice. I'd like you to go up there and run things for the next month. That will help you with your résumé and get us through the end of this year's session."

Camp Touchdown was the family foundation's pet project.

a camp in the Texas Hill Country that provided teens from poor Houston neighborhoods a respite from crime and dysfunctional families. It was an opportunity for them to have a little fun in the sun.

CiCi squealed. "Yes!" This was way better than being the Road Runner mascot. Camp Touchdown was the answer to her prayers. She could spend a good portion of the summer working in her chosen field. She should have thought of it before.

"And you," Texas Bob said to Jake, "are going to help her. You can coordinate the sports and athletics. Your minicamp will be over Friday, so bright and early Saturday morning I want you on your way to the Hill Country. The facility has a complete gym so you can keep in shape. You'll be back in time for Road Runner summer camp and the preseason."

"What in the...what's Camp Touchdown?" Jake asked. "And what kind of athletics are we talking about?"

CiCi answered for her father. "It's a camp run by our family foundation for kids from the inner city. It gives them a chance to get out to the country for the summer. Play sports, swim, canoe, that type of thing. You'd be amazed at how many of those kids think drive-by shootings and heroin are the norm."

JAKE WAS AFRAID to open his mouth; there was no telling what would come out. He'd grown up in the kind of environment CiCi was describing and thanks to football he'd managed to claw his way out.

"Are you talking about juvenile delinquents?" Like his cousins Dwayne and Darrell, the bane of his existence. Being on the bad side of the law was a habit with those two.

"I wouldn't exactly put it that way," CiCi replied.

Of course she wouldn't. The only way Miss Debutante

would run into someone with a rap sheet was if they cut her grass or stole her designer purse.

"Then let me use terms you might understand," Jake sneered. "Are the cops intimately familiar with these brats?"

CiCi gave her father a pleading look. "This isn't going to work."

"Culpepper!"

Jake scrubbed a hand down his face. He'd encountered do-gooders from the "right" side of the tracks before. Every time some church group would show up at his trailer with a box of hand-me-downs or food, Mama would cry when they left. Oh, yeah, those folks were nothing but a pain in the rear.

"Look, I grew up with kids like that. My cousins spent more time in juvie hall than they did at home." Jake didn't bother to mention that he'd also had a couple of minor run-ins with the juvenile justice system.

"I've worked my entire adult life trying to straighten out my relatives, but I haven't been very successful." He shrugged. "At least they're not *permanent* guests of the Department of Corrections, so I guess I've accomplished something. But I have no desire to spend my summer puttin' up with crap like that."

Texas Bob scowled. "If you want to come back to this team, you will. Get my drift, son?"

Yep, he got it. If Jake didn't toe the line, he'd be catching footballs for the worst team in the league.

Damn!

Chapter Four

Jake sank into his overstuffed sofa, a Baccarat tumbler of Johnnie Walker Blue Label in his hands. Tackling the boss's daughter ranked right up there with his all-time worst screw-ups. He was just grateful she wasn't hurt.

Jake was deep in thought when his alarm system beeped, indicating that someone had opened his front door. When he wasn't at the ranch, he lived in an upscale high-rise condo because there was a doorman who was supposed to announce visitors. Obviously the dude was sleeping on the job.

During his football career, Jake had encountered more than a few groupies and they drove him crazy. One time when he lived in the suburbs he'd caught a woman with a camera peeking in his bathroom window. That was one of the main reasons he'd moved to the city.

Jake didn't bother to get up off the couch. If his visitor was a burglar, so be it. Otherwise, very few people had keys to his place—his cousins, his mother and his latest dating mistake, Brenda. And the only reason she had a key was she'd come up with a sob story about needing somewhere to change clothes between her day job and her night classes since her home was too far away. What a mistake that turned out to be. Now every time he asked for the key back, Brenda turned on the water works.

Sure enough, a blonde in a micromini strolled into the

living room as if she owned the place. "Brenda, is the door-bell broken?" Sarcasm wasn't his usual modus operandi, but dammit, she shouldn't be here.

The uninvited visitor sidled up next to him on the couch.

"Jake sweetie, I haven't heard from you in days." Brenda played with the collar of his polo shirt.

He gently moved her hand away. "There's a reason for that. I thought we'd already had this discussion. I don't know how much more blunt I can be. We don't have anything in common and I'm not interested in dating you." Jake didn't want to be cruel, but—

"Oh, baby. You don't mean that." She scooted close and nuzzled his neck. "I was in the neighborhood and thought I'd drop by. You don't mind, do you?"

Jake got up and moved to a chair. "Yes, I do mind." Brenda Olson was a beautiful woman, but she was too clingy for his taste. Too bad he hadn't noticed that when they first hooked up at Cole's barbecue.

So now she had a key to his home and had no qualms about using it.

"I'm leaving town after the minicamp on Friday. I won't be back for a couple of weeks, so why don't you give me back my key. The security company doesn't like to have a bunch of spares floating around." Actually, that wasn't quite true. His security company had no way of knowing how many keys there were, but hey, it was worth a try. Jake hated to make people unhappy, especially when it was a woman who could cry at the drop of a hat.

Brenda stuck out her bottom lip in what she probably thought was a sexy pout. "You're coming back, aren't you?"

"Of course I'm coming back. But you're not. We're through." Jake winced when she picked up the expensive stemware and slammed it on the glass coffee table.

"So in words even a dummy like me can comprehend, you're breaking up with me."

Jake grimaced. She apparently hadn't noticed that he'd used almost those exact words.

"Look, darlin'."

Brenda swatted his shoulder. "Don't look darlin' me, you jerk. I can take a hint." She tossed her mane of golden hair, threw the key at him and flounced out.

Jake stared at door. "This has been a sucky, sucky day," he muttered.

And considering he was about to head off to the backwoods of Texas, the rest of the month was probably was going to get a *whole* lot worse.

Chapter Five

Dinner at the Hurst home was always an experience, but after today's brouhaha, CiCi knew she'd be facing an inquisition.

"CiCi, for goodness' sakes, stop feeding the dog under the table." Mama issued the order without even looking at her daughter. Either she had eyes in the back of her head or she was psychic.

CiCi had thought she and Sugar Plum, the Hurst family Newfoundland, had the covert feeding routine down pat, but apparently not. "Guilty as charged, Mama, but you know I hate broccoli." She was a grown woman, so why should she force herself to eat something she didn't like? After all, she only took a portion of the green stuff to be nice.

Mama frowned at her youngest. "Then do what your nephew does." She waved a fork at six-year-old Wendell Garrison Stockton, III, known as Trip to the family. "Put it in your pocket."

CiCi looked at Trip with new respect. "Wow, is that what you do?"

"Yup." Trip grinned at his cousin Molly.

Mia, the oldest of the three Hurst sisters, gave the kid her best "Mom's not pleased" glare. "That's it, young man. Turn out those pockets. Your dad asked why your jeans always look greasy. Now I know." Mia's husband traveled extensively in his job as an oil company executive.

While Trip was being duly chastised, Marianne continued the conversation. "And, Winston, speaking of Sugar Plum, do you think you could keep her out of the house when I have the bridge ladies over? The last time I had company she drooled all over the mayor's wife's Ferragamos. Needless to say, the old biddy wasn't amused—even though I was." Mama chuckled.

To the casual observer Marianne Hurst might appear to be the quintessential society matron, but she was a rabble-rouser at heart. She just did it in an "oh, so sweet" way.

CiCi rubbed Sugar Plum's belly with her foot and the 125-pound dog responded with a spasm of ecstasy, sending dinnerware skittering across the table.

"Winston, the dog!"

"Yes, darlin'." Winston "Texas Bob" Hurst winked at his daughters and got up to lure Sugar Plum out to the kitchen and her kibble.

Sugar Plum was a food slut. Give her a pork chop and she was your friend for life. Hand over a T-bone and you'd be joined at the hip.

"Hey, brat, why don't you fill everyone in on what happened between you and Jake Culpepper?" Leave it to Mackenzie to bring up the one subject CiCi most wanted to avoid.

Secretly—*very* secretly—she had to admit Jake Culpepper was attractive. But that was on a need-to-know basis, and her sisters were definitely not included in that exclusive group of one.

"Not much to tell. I was dancing around in the costume and the next thing I knew Jake Culpepper was on top of me."

Mac fanned herself. "Just thinking about it makes me hot. That man is a hunk." For some reason, her sister didn't harbor any resentment toward professional athletes, and she certainly had as much reason to as CiCi did.

Marianne cleared her throat. "Remember little pitchers

have big ears. And I thought that you—" she pointed at CiCi "—had sworn off football players. In fact, I distinctly remember you condemning them all to h-e-double toothpicks."

CiCi didn't have a chance to answer before Mia jumped into the conversation. "Seriously, what's he like and did you get hurt?"

"I'm fine, more shaken up than anything. He's big, really big and he looks…" CiCi paused, trying to come up with a suitably neutral description. Anything else would be the equivalent to throwing a ham hock to a pack of frenzied dogs.

"Like a walking-talking sexual fantasy." Mac tossed in her two cents' worth and punctuated it with a giggle.

"Mac!" Mama admonished.

"Seriously?" Mia asked.

CiCi shrugged. Mac was right. "I don't know. I guess. But since Daddy's banishing him to Camp Touchdown for the next month, I doubt he'll be too interested in getting to know any of us."

Mia arched one brow. "Let me get this straight. He's going to Camp Touchdown, and you're going to Camp Touchdown. You'll be there at the same time." She shot CiCi a wicked grin. "That sounds like you'll have plenty of opportunities to 'get to know' each other."

"Stuff a sock in it. I'm not his type." Her sisters with their golden good looks and big hair were probably more his style. CiCi was too tall, too dark and too undebutante. She was the only person in history to flunk out of Miss Newcombe's Finishing School for Young Ladies. Falling flat on her face when she did her debutante court bow was still talked about in certain Houston social circles.

"Children." Marianne addressed the two six-year-olds. "Why don't you give your Mimi some sugar, and then go find Paw Paw and Sugar Plum? Maybe you can talk him into watching you while you go swimming."

Broccoli forgotten, the kids rushed out in a flurry of squeals and giggles.

Mama sighed. "Swear to goodness, I hope your daddy had the sense to keep the dog out of the water. If we lose another pool man because of the hair, I'm going to drain that dratted hole and fill it with dirt." She focused her laser attention on CiCi. "You need to be very, very careful of that young man. He's certainly charming, but he has a reputation with the ladies. We've had enough football-player problems in this family."

CiCi couldn't agree more. "Don't worry, Mama. He wouldn't look at me twice—there's not enough of this." She indicated her AA cleavage. "Plus, I prefer men who settle their problems with words—and it's even better if they're polysyllabic." Although Jake Culpepper's body and bad-boy grin were awfully tempting.

No! She needed to put those thoughts right out of her head. Men were nothing but trouble. Celibacy was definitely the safest way to go.

WHY COULDN'T HE leave well enough alone? Jake thought as he trolled the streets of the exclusive River Oaks neighborhood searching for CiCi Hurst's home. Finding her address had involved a considerable amount of arm twisting and a couple of judicious bribes. He shouldn't be doing this, but he felt he had to talk to Ms. Hurst.

Jake was still driving the pickup from hell. He hadn't had time to go to the ranch to pick up his SUV, and thanks to Dwayne his poor Porsche was toast. Damn—that idiot should be put away for grand theft auto. If only Jake could bring himself to report his cousin to the police.

Why wasn't he an only child? Oh, right. He was. It was his *extended* family that made him crazy.

River Oaks was the crème de la crème of Houston neighborhoods. The houses were palatial, the lawns were manicured and the money was old. It was a world away from the single-wide trailer that Jake had grown up in.

And no matter how much money he had in the bank now, there was always that lingering doubt about fitting in with people for whom debutante balls and Ivy League educations were the norm. Would he use the wrong fork or say something stupid? At least he didn't "chaw" and spit. The same couldn't be said for Dwayne and Darrell.

But tackling that stupid chicken was worse than any social gaffe. That was in the same league as Wrong Way Riegel's scamper into the other team's end zone in the 1929 Rose Bowl.

Jake pulled up in front of a brick colonial that rambled on for at least a block. It had to be bigger than the White House. He checked the address to make sure he had the right place before climbing out of the truck.

No wonder Ms. Hurst still lived at home. Her parents probably had a staff of people ready, willing and able to fulfill her every desire—and apparently a crew of gardeners, too. There wasn't a leaf, a limb or a flower out of place. That is, if he didn't count the gigantic blob smack in the middle of the lawn.

What was that?

When Jake took a closer look and discovered that the mysterious object was a papier-mâché volcano, he almost laughed his butt off. The neighbors were probably already circulating a petition to get rid of it.

Jake paused halfway to the door. More than likely this was a mistake—amend that to he was sure this was a mistake—but he really wanted to talk to Ms. Hurst. So there he was, with his hat in hand, so to speak.

Jake pressed the doorbell expecting to be greeted by a butler in a penguin suit. Instead, he heard a scream and a couple of high-pitched voices fighting over who was going to answer the door.

The little girl obviously won because there she was, complete with a tutu, a tiara and a doll. There was something funky about that doll but Jake couldn't put his finger on it.

"Who are you?" the tiny diva asked. She was holding the doll high enough so the boy standing behind her couldn't reach it. And Jake figured out what was so strange about the doll.

Poor G.I. Joe was wearing a wedding dress and the little boy was trying to rescue him from a fate worse than death.

"Give it back to me!" The kid's squeal was loud enough to peel paint.

"No! Go away!" The girl stuck out her tongue. That was apparently the final straw. A scuffle ensued with no winner, other than G.I. Joe, who was tossed in the corner.

"Uh, kids." Jake tried to get their attention, but they ignored him.

"May I help you?" The honeyed drawl was typically Texan. The face accompanying it was anything but ordinary. Except for her height, she could have easily been a Miss Texas contestant.

"I'm Jake Culpepper." He was about to explain why he was there, but he didn't get a chance to say anything else.

"No kidding!" the blonde beauty squealed.

"Uh, yeah."

"Mia, get a grip."

Jake had been so entranced by the overall drama he'd missed CiCi's arrival on the scene. She looked embarrassed, or chagrined or something.

Before he could figure out what her pink cheeks were all about, another gorgeous woman strolled up. This one he recognized. If memory served, her name was Mac, and she was the assistant coach for the Road Runner cheerleaders. He hadn't realized she was one of Texas Bob's daughters.

"This is Jake Culpepper," Mia announced to the world.

Mac gave him a nod and a wink. "I know. Did you come to see Daddy?"

"No, I wanted to talk to CiCi."

"Me?"

Mac jabbed her sister in the ribs. "Yes, you, dummy," she said with a giggle.

CiCi grabbed Jake's hand and led him out onto the front porch. "Come with me. And you two—" she pointed at her sisters "—close the door."

Mac complied, but not before giving them a finger wave and a hair flip.

"I'm sorry about the ruckus. It gets hectic around here." CiCi didn't bother to squelch her grimace as she led him toward a grouping of white wicker lawn furniture at the far end of the porch. "Let's sit down. So?" Her phony smile was as transparent as a telemarketer's scam.

"I came by to apologize."

"You already did that."

"I know, but I, uh, I don't know. I was afraid I'd hurt you this afternoon." Words had never been Jake's forte. He was much better at letting his actions speak for him.

CiCi made an expansive gesture with her hands. "As you can see, I'm fine."

"That's good. Real good. Since we're going to be working together for the month, I didn't want us to start off on the wrong foot." That was true. But was there another reason he'd driven across town to see her? He'd save that thought for another day.

"Great." She was saying the right thing, but there was something off about her level of enthusiasm. "Friends?" She stuck out her hand.

"Of course." Jake reciprocated.

"Will you come in for a drink? I'm sure Daddy would like to see you."

Was she kidding? Jake would rather face the defensive line of the Chicago Bears without pads than have a drink with Texas Bob. "I think I'll take a rain check." He stood. "Well, I guess that's that." He didn't know what to do with his hands so he stuck them in his pockets. "I can't get up to the camp until Saturday morning, but I guarantee you I'll be there."

"Great," CiCi said again, although her enthusiasm still left a lot to be desired. Then something over his shoulder caught her eye and she looked puzzled. "I wonder why the gardener left his truck here."

Now Jake saw her true colors, and he felt like that kid from the trailer park all over again. He hated it when that happened. "That's my ride." He knew he sounded defensive, but couldn't help it.

"That's yours?"

"Uh-huh."

"Wow, that's, uh…that's really something else." Yep, she was the snob he'd pegged her to be.

"I've gotta go." Jake wasn't about to explain the reason for his vehicle. He started down the steps, then turned and looked back up at her. Since she'd dissed his beater truck he might as well reciprocate.

"By the way, what is that thing?" He indicated the multi-colored lump.

CiCi glanced at the pimple on the landscape. "It's a volcano. The kids are going to science camp and I helped them build it. Now we're trying to figure out how to make it explode without doing permanent damage to the neighbors' windows."

Jake bit back another chuckle. His attempt to rattle her had backfired, but he found he didn't care. "I'll bet that makes you popular with the folks around here."

"We've always been the talk of River Oaks." CiCi leaned

forward as if to share a secret. "They think we're a bit eccentric." Surprisingly she smiled. "See you soon."

Yes, she would. Jake strolled back to his truck and fired up the engine—actually it was more like a cough and a plume of smoke. That should give the people next door, and Ms. Hurst, something to talk about.

Chapter Six

What had she gotten herself into? CiCi wondered as she stuffed clothes willy-nilly into her duffel bag. Jake Culpepper was incredibly good-looking, but acting on that attraction simply wasn't going to happen. Not that he was even vaguely interested in her. She might be rudderless, but dammit, she wasn't stupid.

She was contemplating the sorry state of her life when Mac burst in. Didn't this family know how to knock?

"Are you ready to go?" Mac made herself at home on CiCi's bed.

"Sort of," CiCi replied as she finished zipping her suitcase.

"That Jake Culpepper is a yummy morsel." Mac smacked her lips with exaggerated relish. She might look angelic but deep down she was a devil.

"Really? I hadn't noticed." CiCi's assertion was answered with a undebutante-like snort. Leave it to her sister to raise the BS flag.

"Okay, I confess." CiCi threw herself on the bed and grabbed a bag of M&M's off the nightstand. "I did notice, and yes, he is yummy. But that's where it ends."

"We'll see. Seriously, though, you have to remember he's a hound dog. He changes girlfriends almost as often as he changes his socks."

"I'm always careful." CiCi had learned her lesson with Tank.

"I know. Just keep Tank in mind," Mac said, as she strolled out of the room, taking the candy with her. That girl could be *so* irritating.

Mama stuck her head in the door. "Are you packed?" Why was everyone concerned about her travel plans?

"Pretty much. I have a few more things to do, and then I'm on my way."

Marianne leaned on the doorjamb. It didn't take a Mensa membership to know what was coming next.

"You will take care of yourself, won't you?" That woman could slide into her Mama Bear mode in a nanosecond. Was that character trait handed out in the delivery room?

"I promise I won't swim until an hour after I've eaten." CiCi hid her grin.

"You know what I mean."

She hugged her mom. "I do. And I guarantee I'll be cautious."

Marianne nodded and turned to leave. "Oh, by the way, Sugar Plum's going with you."

It took a second to process that comment. "What?"

"Daddy wants you to take Sugar Plum. He claims she'll be protection." Mama somehow managed to keep a straight face.

"Are you kidding? If that mutt's a watchdog, I'm a supermodel."

"He'll deny it, but I suspect he's going to enjoy a couple of weeks without the dog hair. He's tired of me griping about her clogging up the pool."

AND THAT WAS HOW Sugar Plum ended up riding shotgun in CiCi's chartreuse VW convertible. Making a three-hundred-mile road trip with a humongous black canine, shedding and drooling the whole way, was no picnic. But CiCi was tough, and she was determined to make this work—dog snot and all.

"Hey, Sugar Plum, you want another burger?" she asked during their Sonic Drive-In lunch break. Burgers and dogs didn't mix but CiCi was a softie when it came to those big brown eyes and silly Newfie grin. "I'll take that as a yes." She handed her traveling companion the last sandwich in the bag, being especially careful with her fingers.

"Are you ready?" CiCi pulled out of the parking lot and made her way back to I-10. Little did she know that trouble was brewing, or digesting, as the case may be. They hadn't gone far before the dog's tummy started to rumble. In hindsight, CiCi realized the second burger had been a terrible mistake.

Half a dozen stops later, her patience was wearing thin. "No more Sonic for you, missy." She tapped the dog's black nose. Sugar Plum responded with a doleful look. "See that sign? It says no rest areas for the next hundred and twenty miles. No getting out. No sniffing, no pooping, no nothing. Do you understand?"

CiCi's diatribe was rewarded by a wet doggie kiss across her face. Sometimes she felt like Rodney Dangerfield—she didn't get no respect, not even from woman's best friend.

The flatland of the Texas Gulf coast soon gave way to rolling pastures dotted with native live oak and herds of white-faced Herefords. Shortly before they reached San Antonio, CiCi exited the interstate and headed toward the Texas Hill Country.

Texas back roads were comparable to many states' major highways. That was primarily because they had to accommodate a large number of farm and ranch vehicles, pickup trucks and Suburbans—the unofficial vehicle of Texas. Texans liked their roads wide and pothole free.

CiCi hadn't gone many miles before the landscape changed again—this time to limestone hills, steep canyons, fresh-water springs, vistas of scrub oak and mesquite and lazy meandering rivers. The Texas Hill Country. However, most Texans didn't see the area in terms of geology, mineral production or prehistoric upheaval. To them, it was simply a little piece of heaven.

Back when the state was a republic, the founding fathers decided it was time to settle central Texas and they looked to Europe to entice new residents. They figured if they offered free land, people would come from far and wide. And by gosh, they were right. Seven thousand immigrants from Germany, France, Poland, Czechoslovakia, Switzerland, Denmark, Sweden and Norway came flooding in, bringing a smorgasbord of customs and cultures. But in central Texas, the German traditions had firmly taken root.

The Hill Country had long been a favorite vacation spot for the Hurst family. Mama loved the wineries and boutiques. CiCi was a fan of the bakeries and the ice cream parlor. And Daddy, dear sweet Daddy with his Harvard education, frequented the local bars. He claimed it was research. His theory was there was no better place to get to know his clientele. Almost every summer until she got married, CiCi made the pilgrimage to New Rothenburg, the heart of the Hill Country.

She'd no sooner popped a new Trace Adkins CD in the stereo when she spied her turnoff. Sugar Plum was settled down for a nap, taking up a good portion of the front seat.

Thirty miles down the road, CiCi pulled into a town she knew like the back of her hand. Shiny imports competed with pickups sporting rifle racks for parking spots on the crowded main street.

The sidewalks were packed with tourists, intent on immersing themselves in Bavarian culture—Texas style. CiCi checked out the hordes packing the stores and decided to skip the visit to her favorite ice cream parlor. Blue Belle butter pecan was one of her weaknesses, but today she'd have to pass. Considering Sugar Plum's delicate stomach, it would probably be smarter to go straight to the camp. An ominous rumble came from the canine's tummy—yep, time to haul butt.

Even considering the potential for a gastric disaster, CiCi loved being back in the Hill Country. The Hurst girls had each spent their adolescent summers at Camp Summer Wind on the Guadalupe River. It was during one of CiCi's last years at camp that Daddy had found almost five hundred acres of riverfront property for sale. Eventually that purchase gave birth to Camp Touchdown and the Hurst family foundation, solidifying their connection to her favorite part of Texas.

JAKE WAS ALSO HAVING TROUBLE getting to Camp Touchdown. He'd hit a brick wall when it came to finding Dwayne. When that boy wanted to disappear, he did so with a vengeance. But even a rat had to eventually come out of hiding, and when he did, Jake planned to be waiting.

But that had to be on hold until Jake got back to Houston. For now, he'd be stuck in the middle of nowhere with Miss Debutante and a bunch of juvenile delinquents.

Jake's only consolation was that Ms. Hurst was easy on the eyes—she was a fine-looking woman. But he'd learned a hard lesson about socio-economic snobbery in college when he fell for a society girl and was cut off at the knees for his effort.

CiCi Hurst was off-limits. Even if she'd talk to him after that doozy of a tackle, Texas Bob would *not* be happy if Jake made a move on his daughter. So during his tenure at Camp Touchdown, he'd keep his hands to himself and his libido in check.

With that thought in mind, he pressed on the accelerator. The speed limit on a Texas road might be posted at seventy, but eighty was more the norm.

Once he got through the San Antonio traffic, it was clear sailing to the heart of central Texas. Many years ago, he and Cole had come here for Oktoberfest, but selective amnesia was the order of the day on that trip. That was a case of too much beer, too much wurst and too much of a good thing!

Normally Jake didn't pay much attention to his surroundings, but now he wondered why he hadn't made a return journey to enjoy the countryside. Ancient live oaks and scrub cedar lined the meandering gravel road that led him over Ramada Creek. It was a watering hole for white-tailed deer, wild turkeys, bobcats and numerous diamondback rattlesnakes.

Jake stopped under the heavy crossbeams bearing the Camp Touchdown sign. He lowered his window to listen to the water trickle over rocks as old as time. For some reason he felt at peace. Perhaps he *should* take time to smell the roses, or coffee or whatever the Oprah-ites were suggesting these days. People kept telling him there was life outside football. Could that possibly be true?

And where had all this introspection come from? Jake shook his head as if to clear it of cobwebs—enough of the girly-man stuff. He gunned his brand-new black Dodge Ram with magnum V-8 Hemi. Now *that* was a Texas truck.

Jake had done his homework on Camp Touchdown before leaving Houston. The facility specialized in providing an outdoor experience for inner-city kids, boys and girls ages thirteen to seventeen. There were forty campers at each session. The camp counselors were handpicked from colleges all over the state. Texas Bob recruited budding psychologists, teachers and he even threw in a handful of criminologists for good measure, paying them handsomely for a summer's work.

"Nice," he muttered as he pulled in the front gate. Daddy

Warbucks hadn't spared any expense when he built this place. There were soccer fields, basketball courts, stables and even an Olympic-size swimming pool. An impressive building constructed of native rock with a massive chimney stood guard in the middle of the camp. It didn't look anything like the church camp Jake had attended as a kid.

So he was going to be in charge of sports at this five-star teen resort. Hmm, soccer and basketball he could handle; horses, no way. And if Ms. Hurst thought he was going to teach field hockey or lacrosse, she had another think coming.

Jake's stomach rumbled impressively. It had been hours since his lunch of BBQ brisket, coleslaw, beans and white bread at Oma's Kitchen in Flatonia. He was a growing boy; he needed three squares a day.

Kids were pouring out of the building, giggling, poking each other and generally being obnoxious. And they were heading his way. He'd bet that at least half of them could hotwire a car like a pro. Probably a safe assumption considering he'd learned that skill the summer after the fourth grade.

Jake jumped from the vehicle. "Don't touch the wheels," he told a skinny kid who was edging closer and closer to the Dodge. If they so much as laid a pinkie on the chrome, they'd have to answer to him. Not that he'd really do anything, but he was big and he could look darned scary.

"Hey," Jake called to the tallest boy in the group. The adolescent had leader written all over him. "What's your name?"

The teen put on a great show of disinterest. "Rondelle."

"Okay, Rondelle, I'm leaving you in charge of my stuff." Jake clapped him on the back. "I'm the new football coach, and you look like you'd make a great quarterback."

Rondelle puffed up with pride. "Hey, man, ain't you Jake Culpepper from the Road Runners?"

"Yep."

"Cool. Don't worry, dude, no one will touch a thing. Not without my okay." The teenager poked a thumb at his own chest.

Jake suppressed both a grin and a groan. "Great." He turned to walk away and immediately tripped over a huge dog that had plopped down next to his scuffed boots.

"What the—?" The canine shook its monstrous head and drool flew everywhere.

"Looks like Sugar Plum's in love."

Jake looked for the source of the voice, there she was in the flesh. And what nice flesh it was. Long tanned legs, pixie haircut, twinkling eyes and a pedigree that would choke a horse.

Jake strolled up to where CiCi was standing on the front porch. "Did you say this mountain of fur is named Sugar Plum?" Sugar Plum had plastered herself to Jake's leg and was watching him with doggy adoration.

"That's her name." CiCi cracked a grin. "At least she's not humpin' your leg."

"Thank God for small mercies." Jake scratched behind the dog's ear. "I hate to sound stupid, but what *kind* of dog is she?"

"Sugar's a Newfoundland, but she's had her summer do. When it gets hot, Daddy has the groomer treat her to a buzz cut. It's cooler."

Jake sure hoped Texas Bob wasn't planning to "cut" him, too. Too bad the jury was still out on his chances.

Chapter Seven

Dawn broke much earlier than Jake wanted or expected. "Crap!" He buried his head under the pillow to block the sound of the "William Tell" overture blasting from a loud-speaker outside. When that didn't work, he gave up and pulled his Rolex to eye level. Jeeze, it was too early for even roosters to be awake.

No way was he going to jump out of the bunk. Not that he was comfortable, not by a long shot. His feet hung off the end by at least six inches. It was so narrow, his 260-pound body didn't have room to roll over. And to top it all off, it was hard enough to double as an Aztec sacrificial altar.

Miss Debutante probably had a nice, soft queen-size bed, while he'd been banished to camper hell. Jake groaned as he stood and stretched. This was all part of his punishment, so he'd grin and bear it. In a month, he'd be back to his real life—football, football and more football.

Jake touched his toes, testing his creaking joints. Pain was part of any professional athlete's life—actually, it seemed like an old friend. Humiliation wasn't quite as familiar, and unless he missed his guess, Texas Bob was ready to dish up the crow.

Jake stretched toward the ceiling to work out some of the kinks. He was only thirty, but sometimes he felt as old as

Methuselah. That was the price he paid for being steamrollered by three-hundred-pound tackles day after day.

He hoped to God he'd know when it was time to hang up the cleats. There was nothing more pitiful than a washed-up jock trying to compete with the youngsters and getting killed in the process.

Jake lumbered into the shower. At least he had a private cabin and didn't have to share it with a half-dozen pubescent kids who thought cutting a "silent but deadly" was hilarious.

When he turned on the water he was alternately scalded and frozen by the trickle of water coming from the nozzle. Jake leaned his head against the wall and groaned. This was going to be a *very* long month.

CiCi WAITED AT A TABLE in the dining room for her new athletic director. After three days on the job she finally felt like she was getting her feet on the ground. She just prayed that would translate into being able to manage forty out-of-control teenagers and a staff of twenty randy college students. The entire camp was on hormonal overload.

And speaking of hormones—having Jake Culpepper around 24/7 was disconcerting, to say the least. Just hearing his name made her jittery.

CiCi spooned more sugar into her coffee. He wasn't any different from the teenaged jocks who had made her high school years miserable. They all wanted to date her sisters, but did they ask her out? No way! She was too skinny, too tall and too gawky to register on their testosterone-fueled radar. And unfortunately those long buried teenage insecurities had surfaced when she discovered Tank's adultery.

CiCi was pondering the situation when Mr. Universe sauntered into the dining hall. Every female in the building swooned.

Jake Culpepper's "Wow" factor didn't come from what he was wearing—the shorts, T-shirt and running shoes were nothing special—it was what he looked like that could get him banned in Peoria.

Truly, this was going to be the longest month in the history of mankind.

Jake barely spared his new boss a glance before sauntering over to charm the cook out of a cup of coffee. Even though CiCi had sworn off men, she'd have to be dead not to notice his long, muscled legs and broad chest. He was even wearing a whistle around his neck. The guy was taking his coaching duty seriously.

"If you keep glaring at me like that, you're going to have to have Botox injections to erase the lines," Jake said as he dropped down on the bench next to her. "I thought we'd called a truce. Friends, remember?" He held out his hand.

"Yeah, friends." She hadn't realized she was glaring. Suppressing a mental cringe, CiCi stuck out her hand, totally unprepared for the electric zing that traveled all the way to the top of her head.

The way Jake jerked his hand back, she knew he'd felt it, too, but he had quick reflexes and recovered faster than she did.

He took a long sip of coffee. "We'll be out of each other's way before you know it."

"Yeah, we won't be here long." Uh-huh. "You look tired. Didn't you sleep well?" It was a silly question, but her mind had gone blank.

"The bed's a little short."

"Oh." CiCi hadn't thought about it, but it probably was ridiculous to expect him to fit in a camper bunk. Note to self—order a queen-size bed. "That's one problem I can take care of. I don't want you to be miserable."

"Okay. Why don't you fill me in on what you want me to

do. I can coach football, basketball and baseball, and I can fake it with volleyball. Swimming's not my strength, but I can manage, and horseshoes are a no-brainer." Jake spread his hands in a "that's all there is" motion.

CiCi shook her head in an effort to banish the thought of Jake Culpepper without a shirt. She had never successfully played the boy/girl game and had no idea how to start now even if she wanted to. But naïveté aside, CiCi knew sex appeal when she saw it, and this guy had it in spades. That had to be what was muddying her brain.

"We have a rafting party scheduled for this afternoon. The staff members act as chaperones—you and me included. And I should tell you that while you're on staff, the co-eds are off-limits." Even if that was insulting, she felt compelled to lay out the ground rules. She hoped against hope that his womanizer reputation was overhyped.

Jake put his hands up. "Hey, I'm thirty. Way too old for college girls." He narrowed his eyes. "You really don't have a very high opinion of me, do you?" Her silence was eloquent, but two could play at this game. If she wanted to be snotty, he could be snotty right back. Too bad his libido wasn't cooperating.

The electricity surging between them was almost palpable, but considering who she was, he needed to ignore it. Fortunately, they were interrupted by the arrival of a tall, red-headed guy, who reminded Jake of a young Ron Howard.

"Jake Culpepper. I can't believe you're here. I've watched you since I was a little kid. I'm Greg Anderson, the senior counselor."

Jake visibly winced at his "kid" comment, but shook the guy's hand.

"This is so cool," Greg exclaimed.

The sentiment was obviously shared by the two college girls who had joined the group. They couldn't seem to take their eyes off Jake. That had to be nipped in the bud. Twenty-year-old groupies were nothing but trouble.

"Yeah." The brunette of the duo was the first to regain the power of speech. "Like, this is so sick."

Jake suspected that was a compliment, but he wasn't quite sure.

Greg sat down on the bench, not leaving any room for the girls. It took everything Jake had not to give them his seat. If there was one thing his mother had taught him it was manners. But this wasn't the time to encourage any sort of attraction, so he remained seated. Even so, he felt like a big goober.

Chapter Eight

Jake turned his attention to Greg. "I need to find a running route. Would you be willing to go with me?"

"Sure. How many miles?"

"Five if it's hilly. Ten if I have to run on the flat. The Road Runner summer camp starts in a month and I have to keep in shape. I'm not as young as I used to be."

"Cool. How about starting this morning?" Greg asked.

"Sounds like a plan to me. I just need to change into my running clothes."

"See you in thirty," Greg said with a grin.

A good run was a great way to clear a guy's brain. And since temptation was probably going to be his constant companion, Jake needed his wits about him. What was it about CiCi Hurst that made him want to howl at the moon?

Whatever it was, he had to get over it pretty damned quick. Texas Bob wouldn't be amused if Jake made a play for his "baby girl." Besides, and this was a huge caveat, chicks with trust funds that could pass for the GDP of a small nation were *not* his cup of tea.

It was almost noon when Jake finally wandered down to the river, lured by the sounds of adolescent fun. CiCi had said they were going river tubing today. He wished there had camps like this when he was a kid, trying to keep body and soul together in a neighborhood overrun with felons and crack dealers.

There was no sense in bemoaning a misspent adolescence. It was his adult life that was important, and overall he was doing quite well.

Today was one of those summer days made for lolling about in a hammock with a cold beer and a soft, sweet-smelling female. But Jake had no hammock, no cold beer and the sweet-smelling female would geld him if she got the chance. So he'd go tubing, and by gosh he'd enjoy it. Even if his companions were a bunch of wannabe car thieves.

The cold, green water of the Guadalupe River made its way to the Gulf of Mexico through sheer limestone cliffs, past shrub cedar and live oaks, then meandered through pecan and peach groves. And in the process it provided a playground for tourists and locals alike.

The calm currents hid the violence it could show when the rains pounded the Texas Hill Country. In this part of the world Mother Nature had been known to pitch a hissy, and when she did, smart people sat up and listened. But not today. This was a perfect summer day.

Dozens of truck-size inner tubes were stacked up, surrounded by giggling girls and cocky boys. They were getting last-minute instructions and being fitted for life jackets. Several tubes were tied together to create a floating snack table with coolers of soft drinks and waterproof containers of chips. It looked like an aquatic cocktail party, without the cocktails or napkins.

Jake grabbed the largest tube he could find, but quickly discovered there wasn't a life jacket big enough for him. That wasn't a problem; he knew how to swim. Jake hoisted the tube over his shoulder and elbowed through the crush of teenagers to the dock to wait for Madame Taskmaster, aka CiCi Hurst.

It wasn't long before he spied her over the sea of kids. She was taller than most of the boys, and in her high-cut, black one-piece swimsuit, she was stunning—not touchable, but very attractive. If anything, her choice of attire highlighted the social gulf between them. Her designer suit said she was sorority, debutante court and Junior League, while he was street hockey, Pop Warner football and the barrio.

By anyone's standards that wasn't a good mix. She probably enjoyed literary discussions, caviar and Dom Perignon. He was more comfortable with a Budweiser, nachos and sports. So where did that leave them?

The answer to that was a great big nowhere.

"Hi." CiCi raised her hand. That was the best she could do. No wonder all the co-ed counselors, not to mention most of the female campers, were gaga over Jake Culpepper. In a word, he was hot. HOT!

It was a darned good thing he was wearing a T-shirt because she suspected that one look at his world-class chest would leave her drooling, addlepated and incapable of coherent conversation. Just thinking about it sent her skittering back to her post-divorce mantra—remember Tank, remember Tank.

"I see you're all set." Swimsuit, inner tube, standing by the water—yep, he was ready to roll. "Okay, let's do it."

It was time to get down to business. CiCi signaled the staff to join them for a prefloat meeting. While the college kids were ambling over, she decided to ask Jake a question that had been on her mind ever since Daddy had ordered him to the camp.

"Are you sure you're up for this?"

"Yes, ma'am." He touched the brim of his Texas Rangers ball cap.

Why did he have to be a gentleman? If he acted like a jerk, it would be so much easier to ignore him.

"Well, good." What else could she say, other than she hoped he enjoyed burned hot dogs.

"Is everyone ready?" The staff members nodded. "Great. Cookie and her team will drive down to the dam and set up our picnic."

"Are we having s'mores?" That question was asked by a pudgy counselor who clearly hadn't missed too many meals.

"Yes, we are," CiCi assured him. "We're doing kid food. I suspect this crew will attack the cuisine like locusts ploughing through a field of new wheat. Let's get moving." CiCi crossed her fingers and gave her senior counselor a thumbs up.

It would take nearly two hours to float to the dam. From there the itinerary included food, swimming and some organized games before they took the kids back to Camp Touchdown in vans.

Greg blew his whistle and the kids stampeded for the inner tubes.

JAKE TILTED his ball cap down and closed his eyes, ignoring the squeals and occasional splashes. The river had a way of soothing the soul. It had been a restless night and the gently lapping water was putting him to sleep.

The respite didn't last long. Rondelle and some of his buddies floated up and bombarded him with questions. What was it like to be a pro athlete? Did he take steroids? Was it true he'd dated half of the Road Runner gals? The answers ranged from great, to absolutely not, to a quarter maybe, but definitely not half the cheerleaders.

A skinny carrot-topped stringbean paddled over to join the interrogation. "Hey, man, how 'ja make it to the big time?"

That was a good question. The truth was that it had taken

a combination of phenomenal luck, athletic genes inherited from his absentee father, hard work and Aunt Pallie's prayers. But how much of that would sink in with kids who thought work was a four-letter word?

"I stayed off drugs, put my nose to the grindstone and kept out of trouble." Too bad the same couldn't be said for his cousins. "I started playing football when I was in middle school," Jake continued, thinking that if he could interest even a couple of these boys in sports, his sojourn in the back country might be worthwhile.

"I bet you got yourself a whole pile of money." That insight came from a kid with a shock of dyed bright green hair that stood straight up from his otherwise shaved head.

Great fashion statement, but Jake wasn't about to discuss his finances with his floating companions.

"Not everyone in pro sports is rich." He was, but he wasn't willing to share that with the young felons. "The important thing is to find something you like and do it well. So that means studying, working out and finishing things you start." When had he turned into a philosopher?

Jake paddled over to the float, carrying the cooler. "Would you guys like a soft drink?" He held up a frosty can.

There were enough raised hands to start an Amen Chorus. Jake handed out the drinks and popped the top of his own can. "Be sure to put the empties back in the raft. I mean it— throwing them in the river isn't an option." Jake sympathized with the plight of these kids. Heck, it hadn't been all that long since he was one of them. But that didn't mean he was going to go easy on them. If he had to spend his summer with a bunch of juvies, they'd have to shape up.

Rondelle nodded and his cohorts followed suit.

"Tell you what," Jake said. "After we eat we'll have a shirts and skins game. I'll teach you some basic moves. When you go back to school, you'll be one up on the rest of your friends."

That idea was apparently a hit. The kids floated away in a flurry of pokes and insults. Jake shook his head, thinking about his cousins and how they'd never grown up. He hoped these guys wouldn't share the same fate.

"I see you already have a fan club." While Jake was lost in thought, CiCi had paddled up and grabbed his inner tube to keep them together in the fast-moving current. Sugar Plum had her own raft. Wouldn't you know it, the pup didn't know how to dog paddle.

"You should be wearing a life vest," CiCi said, looking at him over the top of her sunglasses. "It's not a good example for the kids. Not when I force them to obey the rules. Needless to say, they don't think life vests are cool."

Jake hadn't thought of that. "Sorry. I couldn't find one that fit."

"Oh, right. Before our next water activity, I'll see if I can get you an extra-large ski vest. That should do the trick." Ski vest, chest—yikes! She was back to that shirtless thing again.

He touched her arm. "You'd better watch out, princess. You're awfully pink. It looks like you're getting sunburned. Do you feel all right?"

"I'm fine. Thanks. I have some sunblock in here." Little did he know it was a blush, not a flush. CiCi patted a mesh bag that was tied to her inner tube before she paddled off.

Jake briefly wondered what that was all about, but ultimately decided that deciphering the female thought process was too scary to contemplate. So, it was back to his cat nap.

He was half asleep when he heard what sounded like a party. When their convoy of makeshift rafts and inner tubes rounded a bend in the river, Jake discovered there was a shindig going on.

He'd heard from Greg that the dam was the happenin' place. The rumor had it that this was the Hill Country's version of a theme park, and as usual the college kids had it pegged.

People of every description were milling around the dam, waiting their turn to slide into the rushing current. The sliders ranged from skinny to fat, young to old and tattooed to buff. And from the looks of things they were having a good time.

One by one the campers hopped out of the inner tubes and scampered up the bank to the picnic area—food first, sliding later. It was amazing to see the way they could ditch their streetwise bravado and enjoy being kids. If that feeling could be captured and made to last, the juvenile criminal justice system would shut down.

Unfortunately, these idyllic days were limited, outnumbered by others filled with drive-by shootings, welfare and rap sheets. But life was impossible to predict. By all rights, Jake should be doing twenty to life in Huntsville instead of being on a first-name basis with the movers and shakers of Houston. Destiny was a capricious bitch and he hoped that in some small way this time at Camp Touchdown could turn these kids around.

The picnic was an orgy of potato chips, hamburgers, hot dogs, Cokes, homemade peach ice cream and chocolate-covered s'mores. It wasn't fancy or classy but it tasted better than any five-star fare. That cinched it; Jake was a big kid at heart.

With three burgers and almost a gallon of ice cream in his gut, Jake figured a nap was exactly what the doctor ordered so he stretched out under a leafy pecan tree. If CiCi needed him, she'd holler.

Chapter Nine

"It's time to earn your keep, big guy." Jake woke to the sound of CiCi's voice and the feel of her toe nudging his knee. Sugar Plum joined the fun by giving him a slurpy dog kiss. Yeew! Jake wiped his face with the hem of his T-shirt. That dog was a big drool machine.

"You're not supposed to exercise after eating. It'll give you cramps," he replied, not bothering to raise the brim of his cap.

"Oh, please. That's just an old wives' tale." CiCi sounded so annoyed he opened his eyes. She was darned cute all puffed up with righteous indignation.

"What do you need, boss lady?" Jake couldn't resist a grin.

She nudged him again, a little less gently this time. "I think we should play tag football. Come on, be a sport. You can choose your own team. I'll pick mine." That piqued his interest. Jake sat up, returning his baseball cap to its proper position.

"You don't look like a jock to me."

Her innocent "who me?" grin was a dead giveaway. It was a good thing he could spot a shark a mile away. He stood to take full advantage of his size.

"So I get first choice, right?"

"Nope, ladies first."

His intuition was bang on. She'd been scouting while he napped. But he didn't intend to lose. Wile and cunning counted for a lot in football. And he was pretty good at ferreting out talent, even if he did say so himself.

"Okay, princess. You pick first. But you didn't answer my question about being a jock." He wanted to know up front what he was facing.

CiCi's grin went from innocent to wicked. "I played NCAA Division I volleyball. I even made it to the Olympic trials." She shrugged. "I didn't make it, but hey, that's world-class sports. And you should never underestimate the power of a determined woman."

Jake had learned that lesson the hard way, starting with his mom and continuing with groupies wanting him to autograph their unmentionables.

CiCi waved at a group of kids waiting on the field. "They're ready for us. Remember, I get first pick. And you have to choose some girls. No one gets left out."

"I got it." Jake lagged a few steps behind. The view of her rear was stupendous. Jake considered himself a connoisseur of fine derrieres, and hers was mighty fine. In his opinion, legs were eye-catching and breasts were enticing, but there wasn't anything like a firm, round butt.

Oh, man! That kind of thinking was gonna get him into a world of hurt. Everyone knew that debutantes didn't hook up with guys from the projects unless they were out slumming. She didn't seem like much of a party girl, but what did he know? And anyway, her daddy could get him banished to the last-place team in the league. *That* was his idea of football hell.

Jake couldn't figure out what made CiCi Hurst tick. Sometimes she acted as if she wasn't sure what to think of him, but at other times he thought he saw her eyes light up when she looked at him.

CiCi had produced a basket of T-shirts and hankies for the touch-football game. "Okay, kids, Jake's team will be yellow and mine will be red. Tuck the hankie in your back pocket. Absolutely no tackling. Hear me? No tackling. When the opposing team gets your hankie, you're down," she instructed. The players nodded their understandings. "Good. I pick Jason." CiCi pointed at one of the tall, well-built camp counselors.

Jake was right. She'd scouted. He'd been planning to pick Jason first. The guy was big and buff, and obviously played ball at school.

He studied the talent pool and made his choice. "Okay, Rondelle, you're my man." Even if they didn't score a point, the kid's ear-to-ear grin was enough to make Jake happy with his decision.

The selection went back and forth. Both Jake and CiCi were careful to pick the kids who were probably used to being passed over.

Jake was putting a great deal of thought into his next draft when a light tap on his arm drew his attention. He was still pondering whether he should grab Javier before CiCi realized his potential, or punch up his defensive line with a husky guy named Alvin.

It took a few seconds for Jake's brain to segue from beefy linebackers to golden-haired angels. And the young lady trying to get his attention could have posed for Botticelli. She had spun-gold curls, cornflower-blue eyes and was no bigger than a minute even though she had to be at least fifteen. Soaking wet, the girl couldn't weigh more than a hundred pounds.

She got up on tiptoe to whisper in his ear. "Coach, I want to play."

"Are you sure?" The last thing they needed was for someone to get hurt, especially one of their younger campers.

"Positive. I'm the kicker on our varsity team. I'm an okay

punter, but I'm really accurate with field goals and points after touchdowns."

Jake couldn't have been more surprised if she'd smacked him in the face with a wet fish.

"You are?"

"Sure, I'm also a cheerleader and I play soccer, but during the game when they need me, I whip on some pads and a helmet and go out and kick bootie."

Jake barely suppressed a grin. "How about that? Okay, what's your name?"

"Angel."

That figured.

"Angel's my next pick," he announced loudly. He couldn't wait to wipe the smirk off Ms. Hurst's face. He'd be willing to bet a future Super Bowl ring that she didn't have a kicker. Little Angel was going to be his ace in the hole.

After they finished picking teams, Jake called his squad over to huddle. "Rondelle, have you ever thrown a football?" With Rondelle's height and athleticism, he was a natural for quarterback. Plus, he was a born leader.

"Sure. I played on the middle-school team."

Jake didn't miss the use of the past tense. He wondered why Rondelle wasn't currently playing. For a project rat, sports could be a godsend. And if ever someone needed a miracle, Rondelle qualified. But first things first—right now they had a football game to win.

Jake checked out the talent. One of his girls was built like an offensive tackle. If she could block, that would be a bonus. About half his team had played ball at some point in their lives. For the neophytes, Jake explained snap counts, simple plays and the importance of getting the ball over the chalk line.

"Rondelle, throw the pigskin over everyone's head and I'll catch it. And keep it away from Sugar Plum. I think she's on the other team." Jake wasn't sure it was fair for him to play, but CiCi had thrown down the gauntlet. Losing wasn't an option.

"Right on, Coach," Rondelle yelled, giving his teammates a high five.

Unfortunately, enthusiasm didn't equal skill and the first series of downs was a disaster. Rondelle tried handing off to his running back, a kid with an amazing punk haircut who immediately dropped it. After a mad scramble, Jake's team recovered the ball. That was followed by loopy Hail Mary that even a pro football receiver wouldn't have caught. The next calamity was a bobble from the center to the quarterback. That's when Jake played his trump card—Angel. She punted the ball a mile, pushing the other team back toward their end zone.

How about that!

It was time for some team spirit. "Don't worry—they don't have a chance," he said. "Everyone gather around. Who's gonna win?"

The resounding "we will" gave him hope. Now, if he could keep his eyes off CiCi and her smartly curved rump they might pull this off.

They had decided on a half-hour game and at the end of it, Jake's team was ahead, thanks to Angel's last-minute field goal.

That girl could kick. She was probably a killer on the soccer field.

CiCi performed the requisite coaches' handshake but under her breath she muttered, "Don't gloat or I might have to smack you."

Although she smiled when she said it, Jake didn't think she was joking. He didn't know her well, but if she was anything like her daddy, she was competitive as all heck.

He put his arm around her. "Let's take the kids over to the dam. Sliding looks like a lot of fun."

FROM HER OWN YEARS at camp, CiCi could attest to the entertainment factor of dam sliding. "Sure, we have about forty-five minutes before the vans pick us up. Do you have your whistle with you?"

Jake reached in his pocket and pulled out the symbol of his coaching authority. "I wouldn't be without it." He put it in his mouth and issued a quick blast.

When everyone had gathered around, CiCi said, "Grab your life vests and head to the dam. You have forty-five minutes. If I see you without a vest, you're out of the water." She shot the group a glare. "Got it?"

Sometimes she worried she was too strict, but these kids were her responsibility.

"Yeah!" The kids gave a collective scream before they scrambled toward the pile of life vests. Why was it that when kids were involved, pandemonium was the name of the game?

It took mere seconds for the racket to subside and the hordes to disperse.

Jake watched as the campers scattered toward the dam. "I think your idea was a big hit."

"Absolutely." CiCi couldn't wait to do some sliding herself. "Race you." The minute the words left her mouth she knew she'd made a mistake. The man ran for a living, and he was darned good at it.

"How about the winner gets to name the prize?" His grin was positively lascivious.

Bad, bad idea. "Sure," CiCi said, then immediately wondered where that had come from.

She gave him a shove and took off, knowing that unless he'd landed on his keister, she didn't have a chance of winning. And sure enough, there he was passing her with a cheeky wave.

Chapter Ten

Flip the pillow. Roll over. Check the clock.

Punch the pillow. Throw off the sheet. Check the clock.

Insomnia sucked! It had been a long day and CiCi was dead tired, but when she closed her eyes all she could see was Jake Culpepper's glorious body.

Was it too late to call Mac's cell? Eleven o'clock was marginal, but she decided to risk hearing her big sis gripe. After all, CiCi was having a minicrisis.

The phone rang half a dozen times before Mac croaked out an exasperated, "What do you want?"

"Did I wake you?"

Mac answered with a grunt. She didn't sound too happy.

"Hey, I'm sorry. I couldn't sleep."

"Oh, really." Apparently, her sisters default setting was sarcasm. "Spill it."

CiCi heard the sound of a creaking headboard and a pillow being fluffed up. "It's Jake Culpepper."

"And?"

"I'm confused. He's irritating as all heck and he's the last thing I need, but I'm still tempted to throw him down and ravage him."

Mac giggled, then chuckled and finally broke into a hearty laugh. "*Ravage* him?"

"That's it. I'm not calling you again." CiCi was about to punch off.

"Hey, silly. Don't hang up, please. I'm sorry. But you have to admit it's funny. Miss I'm Going to Be Celibate the Rest of My Life is discussing ravaging someone."

"It's not *that* funny." CiCi wanted to pout, but couldn't quite manage it.

"Oh, but it is. And what's wrong with being attracted to a handsome man? Is he nice?"

"Yeah, he is," CiCi admitted, then immediately wanted to change the subject. Which was ridiculous since she'd called Mac specifically to get some advice on what to do about Jake. "Did I tell you that we floated down to the river dam for a picnic?"

"I love that place," Mac said. "And then what happened?" She was definitely grinning.

"We divided up the campers and played tag football." This conversation was making CiCi hungry. She rummaged through her small refrigerator, looking for a snack. A can of Mountain Dew, a carton of strawberry yogurt and half of a leftover sandwich—nope nothing looked appealing.

"Did his team win?" Mac asked. Now that she was awake, that girl could talk for hours.

"Yes, darn it. But the only reason was he had a five-foot-nothing blond cheerleader who could probably kick for the pros. She made the winning field goal." CiCi finally settled for a glass of ice water. She made a mental note to raid the downstairs kitchen later.

"He's single, isn't he?" Mac was good at getting to the heart of the matter.

"I'm pretty sure he is, but I'd bet my trust fund that he has his own little harem of female fans."

Mac was quiet for a few seconds before conceding the issue. "I've heard a couple of rumors but I don't know if they're true." Like CiCi, she was intimately familiar with the problem of groupies. Her extremely handsome pro quarterback ex-husband had had women following him as if he was the Pied Piper.

"Why don't you give him a chance?" Mac asked. "What could it hurt? All you have to do is be nice and see what happens. You certainly don't have to marry him."

Her sister was right. Even if they never dated, they had to get along or this was going to be the longest month ever. As long as she could keep her attraction under wraps, everything would be okay.

CiCi wasn't the only person with insomnia. Jake swatted a mosquito and uttered vile curses, all related to Texas Bob's parentage. He'd kill for a cold beer and a hot shower. Instead he had a lumpy cot and rain-forest humidity. Plus the damned bullfrogs never shut up. The air-conditioned lodge with its working shower was sounding more and more like heaven. He hadn't been this miserable since middle school, when he'd had to share a bunk bed with Dwayne.

A drop of sweat rolled down his chest and nestled in the center of his belly button, quickly followed by a second. Would Ms. Hurst bust his chops if he went skinny-dipping? Probably. She was undoubtedly sitting up there in her air-conditioned splendor, plotting ways to zing him.

The familiar low rumble of a truck engine interrupted his mental diatribe. He jumped out of bed and into his jeans and a T-shirt, not bothering to zip his pants. Swear to God if those juvies broke the ignition on his Ram, he'd kill them with his bare hands. Without pausing for shoes, Jake roared out the door and sprinted toward the parking lot.

Sure enough, the little morons were trying to steal his truck. Rondelle was in the driver's seat and his cohorts in crime, Javier and Schultz, were about to hop in—that is until

Jake grabbed them and held them up like a couple of fish on a hook.

"That ignition better be intact." Jake shook his captives to emphasize his point. "Rondelle, turn off the engine and get out," he said through gritted teeth.

Rondelle obviously knew when someone meant business. He emerged from the truck with his hands in the air. Good grief! The teen had either been busted before or he watched too much Court TV. "Hey, man, we weren't gonna take it nowhere. We's just havin' a little fun."

Jake resisted the urge to rattle the kid's teeth. That's what he got for being a nice guy. Did Rondelle really want to get sent back to the hood?

"You two sit right there and don't move a muscle." He dropped his captives. They fell to the ground, nodding like bobble-head dolls.

"And you—" he pointed at Rondelle "—assume the position. I'm going to search you for weapons." With Rondelle's attitude, a little scare couldn't hurt.

By the time he finished frisking the teenager, CiCi had arrived on the scene.

"What in the world is going on out here?" Sugar Plum had followed her out and was barking and bouncing around like a Jack Russell Terrier on speed. Pretty soon everyone in the camp was going to be involved.

Jake was momentarily distracted by CiCi's tiny tank top and pair of boxer shorts, but forced his attention back to the business at hand.

"Our buddies decided to go for a joy ride," he told her. "In my truck!" Just then Sugar Plum sniffed his crotch. "Jeeze, I hate that."

CiCi avoided looking at him. "Um, do you think you could do something about that?" she said, waving a hand in the general vicinity of his jeans. "Your zipper's…uh…it's at half-mast."

Jake looked down. Damn, she was right. He yanked up the zipper. How about that? A little problem like that wouldn't bother her unless she was interested.

"Thanks. So what do we do about this? I don't want to call the sheriff, but—" she'd moved close enough that she could whisper "—I think they need to understand the ramifications of breaking the law."

"Ramifications of breaking the law? They were about to steal my truck. Why are you bothering to pretty it up?" Then it hit him. "You studied psychology, didn't you?"

"Yes."

"And you think all they need is some hand-holding and a couple of stanzas of 'Kumbaya'." Jake really tried to keep the sneer out of his voice but knew he didn't quite succeed.

"I wouldn't say that."

"So what *do* you want to do with them?"

"I, uh, I don't exactly know."

"Then let me take care of it. If you don't like my methods, you can fire me." For Jake that was a win/win situation. He reached into the truck and turned on the headlights. "You three, plop your butts right there in the light. Don't move a muscle. Got it?"

The miscreants nodded in unison and shuffled over to where they were told.

"Let me look at something." Most new cars were impossible to hot-wire, so how had they started it? Dammit, the key was in the ignition. Why did they have that?

Jake jerked it out of the ignition and went over to confront the little felons. "How did you get this?" Jake was ready to thump them, no matter how hard CiCi glared at him. What did she expect him to do?

Javier and Schultz turned to Rondelle but didn't say a word.

"Rondelle!"

The teen looked sheepish, but tried to cop an attitude. "I heisted it out of your cabin."

"Wrong answer, kid." Jake's voice was deadly soft. "I've dealt with people a lot tougher than you."

He motioned for CiCi to go with him to the tailgate. "I am so mad I could spit nails. Stand here with me until I calm down," Jake muttered so the boys wouldn't hear him.

"Okay."

Jake took two deep breaths to slow his heartbeat. "I have an idea. Are you willing to play along?"

"I won't let you hurt them."

So much for their truce. "I have to tell you, princess, that comment pisses me off. What do you take me for?"

"I'm sorry," she apologized. "That was uncalled for."

Jake searched her expression but she seemed to be truthful. "Damned straight. All right, I forgive you." He shot her the grin he'd patented in the third grade—the one that was guaranteed to get him out of trouble.

"I'm not thinking of any corporal punishment, just some old-fashioned hard work. My life of crime came to a screeching halt when old man Turner caught me trying to steal his Chevy. I worked five of the longest weeks of my life." Jake chuckled, thinking about his summer of servitude. It hadn't seemed funny then, but now he was grateful for the old man's methods. "Believe me, that was when I discovered crime didn't pay."

"How old were you?"

"Ten." He gently tapped her chin when her jaw dropped. "Better close your mouth. You're gonna catch flies. There's nothing quite as disgusting as hand mowing six acres of grass in a San Antonio summer. It gives a kid time to reflect. And I think the irrigation system you've been talking about would be a good place for these guys to start."

He leaned around the truck to look at the perpetrators again. They looked as if they were about to pee their pants. "I think these kids are retrievable. They're just lacking supervision and a stable home life. But that's out of our control." From Jake's experience, tough love was the only thing these teens would understand.

CiCi checked out the kids. "Okay, have at it. But don't scream at them."

"I don't scream. My way is much more effective." Jake grinned as Sugar Plum plopped on his bare feet. "Hey, guys, get your butts over here. I have a deal you won't be able to refuse."

Chapter Eleven

It was almost midnight before the camp returned to normal. Under ordinary circumstances, CiCi loved the night sounds—the cicadas, the bullfrogs and the crickets. Not tonight. She was restless and it didn't take a Ph.D. to figure out why—Jake Culpepper. He wasn't very sympathetic with the kids. Did that translate to all his relationships? Was this another trait he shared with her ex? Tank didn't even know the meaning of the word *empathy*.

CiCi finally gave up trying to sleep. She pulled on a pair of shorts and a tank top and wandered down to her favorite bench by the river. From that vantage point she could see the water and enjoy the sounds of summer. Here in the heart of Texas the skies seemed limitless and the stars were a glorious light show. She loved this place.

"Where I grew up the city glare blotted out the stars," Jake said, making himself at home on the other end of the bench a few minutes after she'd settled in. "That's one of the reasons I enjoy my ranch so much. I like to grab a cold brew and go out on the porch to watch the heavens."

CiCi should have been surprised to see him, but she wasn't. "You can't see the stars in Houston, either." She turned to face him. "Are you having a hard time sleeping?"

"The bed's too small. My feet hang off the end," Jake said with a laugh.

"I'm sorry. Those bunks were made for kids. I never factored in how tall you are, but you'll be glad to know that I ordered you another bed."

"Hey, that's cool. You didn't have to do that, but I appreciate it. I've made do with worse."

"But you don't need to." She felt bad that not only had he been "sentenced" to a month at camp, he was also forced to be uncomfortable while he was there. She wasn't exactly sure how to phrase her next comment but she gave it a go. "You've been a trouper. I'm impressed."

Jake laughed. "It must not take much to impress you. Where were you when I was trying to get a prom date?"

"You think yours was bad, let me tell you about my prom." When CiCi finished telling the tale of being ditched at the dance so her date could neck with another girl in the parking lot, they were laughing so hard she had to wipe the tears from her eyes.

"It sounds better than my date. I was going with Carmelita Schmidt and I worked my tail off to get enough money to make it a special night. But she ended up leaving the dance with her old boyfriend. It sounds a lot like your experience."

It was obviously an embarrassing story, but Jake told it so wryly that CiCi had to giggle.

"Since then I've gotten better with my technique," he added.

She'd just bet he had. Both Mia and Mama had warned her that he was a "player," and CiCi could easily believe it. She remembered numerous pictures of him in the paper with a different woman on his arm each time. She shouldn't—couldn't—let herself relax around him like this. So back to her mantra—remember Tank. Remember Tank. Remember Tank.

When CiCi opened her mouth, she wasn't prepared for

what popped out. "Did you know that I was married to Tank Tankersley?"

"Are you kidding?" Jake looked at her as if she'd grown another head.

"It's the truth." She knew she sounded defensive, but couldn't help it.

"Hey, I didn't mean anything bad, I'm just blown away. I got the feeling that you weren't all that impressed with jocks. And Tank's such a...tank."

CiCi laughed at the accuracy of Jake's description. "He left me for a librarian."

"Are you foolin' me?"

"Nope. It's the honest-to-God truth. Sometimes I wonder if she's into some kinky stuff." CiCi didn't know what made her share that part. That was something she hadn't even told her sisters.

"So how long were you and Tank together?" Jake asked. His expression was uncharacteristically serious.

"Six years."

"Wow. I hadn't heard Tank was married. He was quite a—" He must have realized he was about to stick his foot in it because he did some impressive backtracking. "Not that I was ever friends with him, or anything. In fact, I barely know him."

"Don't worry. I know what Tank is like. I'm fine with everything." That wasn't entirely true but it would have to do. "How about you?"

"I'm not married, no kids, no entanglements. I'm just a lonely soul." He grinned at that obvious lie.

"Uh-huh."

"What time do you have?" Jake asked, holding up his watch. "Mine's not working." Why was that important? It wasn't as if they had anywhere to go.

And why was he sitting so close? They weren't on a date or

doing anything intimate. On the contrary, they were simply sitting by the river, enjoying the evening. But somehow it felt like a dangerous game of foreplay.

Jake leaned across as if to look at the face of her watch, but instead his head kept going and to her amazement he laid a feathery kiss on her bare midriff.

"Oh!" CiCi's breath hitched as her fingers involuntarily stroked the silky hair at the nape of his neck.

When he raised his head, he had the look of a man on a mission—sensual and intent. He was so close that in the moonlight she could see flecks of blue in his green eyes.

"Jeez," he muttered, before lowering his lips to hers.

Although the kiss was almost whisper-soft, it was the most erotic touch CiCi had ever experienced. When Jake explored the seam of her lips, her temperature spiked all the way to the Milky Way. Breathing became impossible, and that was before he deepened the kiss.

She'd known Jake less than a week and she was already on a hormonal overload. What was it about this man that she couldn't resist? Her heart wondered if someone who could kiss like this might be worth the risk. Her head told her to run. So which was going to win—head or heart?

Before things went any further, Jake pulled back. And thank goodness he did because CiCi had totally taken leave of her senses.

"Why did you do that?" God, she hated being a shrew, especially after that kiss, but the very last thing she wanted was to be another notch on his bedpost.

"Because I wanted to." He seemed baffled by her question, and why not? She was definitely overreacting. It was just one kiss. Not the end of the world.

"Wrong answer." She shook her head. "This can't happen again."

Jocks sucked. Players sucked. Remember Tank. Jocks have groupies. Now if she could mentally run that tape when Jake was around, she'd be in business.

Chapter Twelve

Shortly after breakfast, Jake and Greg took last night's wannabe car thieves out for a ditch-digging tutorial. It was hot and humid and the mosquitoes were in fine form. The kids were going to be miserable, CiCi thought as she watched from the shade and comfort of the porch. She was torn between feeling sorry for them and wondering if Jake was right. Perhaps hard work was exactly what they needed.

But what did she need? She pondered that question while sipping her coffee. Floundering around at eighteen was one thing, but doing it at thirty-two was ridiculous.

Enough introspection; there was work to be done. Although she was tempted to watch the chain gang, she'd leave it under Jake's supervision—at least this time. There was more to managing a camp this size than volleyball games, campfires and picnics.

Ordering supplies was high on her To-Do list, but that didn't necessarily require her to stay in the office. CiCi went inside just long enough to grab the cordless phone and Cookie's list of groceries, then went back out on the porch to conduct her business.

The program at Camp Touchdown was more extensive than just sports and crafts. Academic subjects weren't a high priority for most of these kids, so Texas Bob had hired a team of educators to create a curriculum that would make learning fun.

Every morning the classes included a variety of scholastic pursuits, including drama, literature, botany and life sciences. Kids went about collecting insects with a single-minded pursuit that was usually found only in a scavenger hunt. Math was taught by playing poker. And who could forget Shakespeare done with a Texas twang.

The afternoons were dedicated to strenuous activities guaranteed to make the little buggers tired. And today, even Rondelle and his buddies had been released from the chain gang long enough to participate in the softball tourney.

Later that afternoon CiCi was sitting in the bleachers watching the teams play. As hard as she tried, though, she couldn't keep her eyes off Jake. Imagine that?

He was deep in discussion with a nubile young lady named Heather who was the coach of the other team. CiCi realized this was purely professional but that didn't ease the yucky feeling she got when said nubile-ite rested her hand possessively on Jake's back.

CiCi knew better than to trust a man who had access to Sharpie-toting women wanting their boobs autographed.

Okay—she'd truly crossed the abyss to lunacy.

She needed to calm down. He wasn't Tank, and as long as he wasn't consorting with the college staff, whatever he did was his own business.

Sounds of "You Ain't Nuthin' But a Hound Dog" came from deep in her cargo pants' pocket. That was Mac's ring. Her sister normally wouldn't call in the middle of the day so this had to be important.

"What's up?" CiCi asked as she answered.

"You'll never believe this!"

CiCi pulled the phone back from her ear. Mac was loud when she got excited. "What?"

"I had a date with Cole Benavides."

It took a moment for CiCi to comprehend exactly what her sister said, but when she did she almost had a seizure.

"What! Wait, wait, please tell me you didn't say that!" Cole Benavides was the Road Runners' quarterback! What worm had burrowed into Mac's brain?

"I did." She paused. "It wasn't really a date. We met at Starbucks for coffee. I like him." Mac giggled.

Good heavens! Hadn't Mac learned anything from her divorce? Why would she put herself through that kind of grief again? Cole Benavides was the NFL's answer to Brad Pitt. Blond, athletic, charismatic and handsome as sin—he was a heartbreak waiting to happen, and absolutely the last person in the world Mac should get involved with.

"Why are you so quiet?"

What could CiCi say? Other than "are you out of your mind?" As tempting as that was, she couldn't bring herself to be that blunt, so she went with something a little more benign.

"Sweetie, I don't want to be a wet blanket, but you really have to be careful. Guys like Cole Benavides eat people like you for a snack."

There was a pause before Mac let her have it with both barrels. "I hate to tell you this, *sister dearest,* but I'm a grown woman. And I can decide who to see. So considering that I'm really irritated with you right now, I think I'll hang up."

CiCi stared at the phone, hoping her sister would call back, but no such luck.

Life hadn't been easy for Mac and Molly since her sleazy husband left her for his massage therapist. In their more lighthearted moments, CiCi and Mac had laughed at the cliché.

Professional athletes in almost all sports lived in a heady environment. Millions of kids dreamed of going pro but only a tiny percentage ever made it, and those who did faced a unique challenge. Could they keep their priorities straight despite the money, adulation and fame? Tank had succumbed to an adulterous affair, as had Mac's husband. What about Jake? Did he have his head on right? She didn't know him well enough to answer that question.

That was a hurdle they'd never be able to get over. She'd known too many athletes who'd lost sight of common sense to ever get involved with another one.

Chapter Thirteen

It had been a long, hot, sweaty day and Jake was on his way back to the cabin for a cool shower. Amazingly, Camp Touchdown was growing on him. He'd only been there a couple of days and he was already getting used to the smell of newly mown grass, the sound of the cicadas nestled in the live oaks and the nonstop teenage noise.

Overall, Jake was content—that is, until he thought about CiCi Hurst. He'd dated some of the most beautiful women in Texas, but something about her appealed to him on a deeper level than "wow, she's a hottie."

Unfortunately, the feeling wasn't reciprocated. Her reaction to his kiss made that quite clear. Why did she have such a low opinion of him? Heck, he could get dozens of people to testify that he was one of the good guys. Even his ex-girlfriends (Brenda excluded) liked him. So what was with CiCi Hurst? Women—you couldn't live 'em and you sure as shootin' couldn't live without 'em.

Since he didn't have a hope in hell of deciphering her thought process, Jake decided to press on to a subject that was more comprehensible—kids. Watching the campers let down their defenses and just be kids was pretty cool.

And if his being here made a difference in even one life, it might just would be worth the cramped quarters, cranky shower and interminable humidity. But that didn't mean he intended to get involved in their lives. Kids like Rondelle and crew were incredibly needy, and like Darrell and Dwayne they would suck the life blood out of him if he'd let them.

Jake was about to strip down to jump in the shower when he heard a racket.

"Jake! Jake, open the door!" CiCi was pounding on the cabin door as if there was no tomorrow. "I need your help."

This time he remembered to zip his jeans before unlatching the screen. "What's wrong?"

"Jennifer, one of the counselors, is in Spiceville and she just called to say that some of our kids are at a pool hall/kid hangout. They're about to get in a fight with the townies."

"Which kids?" Jake asked, even though he'd bet his last dollar he knew exactly who was heading up the pack. "Is it Rondelle and his buddies?" He truly wanted to throttle that kid.

CiCi nodded.

"How did the little jerk have the energy to get in trouble after digging ditches and playing ball all day?"

She shrugged.

Chip, the head counselor of the boys' dorm, sprinted up. "There are five missing campers. Rondelle, Javier, Schultz, Timmy Smith and Shawn. One of the kids said they planned to hitchhike into town to get a beer."

"Terrific," Jake muttered. "They're drinking under age and have probably been mouthing off to the locals. Those idiots have mush for brains."

"Do we have a vehicle big enough to bring them all home in?" CiCi addressed her question to Chip.

"Just the gardener's truck. We could load them in the back and hope someone doesn't fall out."

That was neither optimal nor safe—and it definitely wasn't legal—but desperate times called for desperate measures. And keeping the kids from getting beat up trumped everything.

"Why don't you go get the truck and we'll head in to town to retrieve them."

"Yes, ma'am, as good as done." Chip sprinted off toward the employees' cabins.

It took almost fifteen minutes for Chip to show up, driving the junker from hell. There was a huge wooden box fixed to the middle of the bench seat, leaving room for only two people to sit—and guess what, there were three of them.

Jake got a suspicious, sexy gleam in his eye. "Looks like you're gonna have to get real cozy with me."

Not likely! But what was her other choice? It was either sit on Jake's lap or share the back with a load of lawn equipment. And would it be all that terrible to get up close and personal with Jake Culpepper?

"I can sit on the edge of the seat," CiCi said, thinking that was a viable alternative. She didn't count on the fact that a 260-pound male filled up more than his share of space.

Jake got in the truck and patted his lap. "Come on, I won't bite."

That part was debatable. She'd sit very lightly. It wasn't that far into town. But when they finally made it to the city limits, her arms ached from gripping the dash. And to make matters worse every time she slid back onto his lap, she felt him chuckle.

"There. I think that's the place." CiCi pointed at a ramshackle building in the middle of a parking lot. It was surrounded by muscle cars, old rattle-traps and pickups with rifle racks. The flickering neon sign announced that this was the home of the Texas Ten-Ball Video and Billiard Emporium.

"Oh, my God." There was no telling what they were going to find. CiCi hoped to goodness it wouldn't involve flashing lights and badges. She was about to ask Jake what he thought when he unceremoniously slid out from under her and jerked the door open.

He was out of the truck and halfway across the pavement before the vehicle came to a stop. CiCi was right behind him. She had obviously missed something important. Then she saw what had grabbed his attention.

The ring of teens partially obscured her view, but she instinctively knew that Rondelle was at the heart of the altercation. The man who was about to pummel him had an advantage of at least ten years and fifty pounds.

CiCi pulled out her cell, ready to call 911. Then the crowd spied Jake and parted like the Red Sea.

"What's happenin' here?" he drawled in a quiet but dangerous tone as he stepped between Rondelle and his opponent. The smart guys hightailed it to their cars when he'd put on his "take no prisoners" voice. Even CiCi was tempted to back up.

"I really don't think you want to find out what happens when you assault a kid, now do you?" He spoke so softly even the crickets had stopped chirping to listen. "So why don't you, and whoever's left of your buddies, call it a night and go on home." Jake backed the redneck up until he was at least ten feet from Rondelle.

In an obvious effort to save face, the man uttered an expletive and stomped off.

Jake waited until the guy was in his pickup before he turned his glare on Rondelle. "You—" he stabbed a finger at the teen's chest "—and your friends get in the truck. We'll deal with you when we get back to camp."

Rondelle's dejected little gang practically tripped over their own feet in their race to the truck.

"I'm not sure what to do next. Digging ditches obviously didn't work," CiCi said.

She, Jake, Greg and Chip were in the kitchen, eating cookies and contemplating their next move. Sugar Plum was trolling the area for crumbs, while the ragtag band of ne'er-do-wells awaited their fate in the dining room—sans Oreos. Personally, Jake was ready to put them on a diet of bread and water.

"If someone would write an owner's manual on teenagers they'd make a fortune. Studying this stuff at school is one thing—living it is something else." CiCi looked as dejected as Jake felt.

"It's especially tough when you're dealing with the kind of boys we have here," Jake said as he made a pot of coffee. "Most of them have had a hard life, and they're desperately looking for structure and role models." He wasn't sure why he was willing to share this observation, but there it was. "The problem is they don't know how to accept it when that's offered to them."

When the coffee gurgled, he stuck a cup under the stream of liquid. "You look like you could use this." He handed CiCi the mug and sat down. "You guys want some?" he asked Chip and Greg, who declined. "Okay, here's my suggestion. I think we should continue with the ditch digging and not make a huge deal out of this. Believe it or not, I think they can be trustworthy if they know what's expected. At the moment, they're testing us, seeing how far we'll let them push the limits. So, we give them very specific rules and tell them exactly what will happen if they misbehave again. Three strikes and they're out, if you want to use sports terminology. Then we sit back and hope to God it works. I really don't think any of them are anxious to go home."

CiCi COULDN'T BELIEVE her ears. Somewhere along the way, Mr. Grump had turned into an expert on dysfunctional adolescents. So he had a Chippendale body, a nice personality *and* intelligence. That was effen' fantastic. She really didn't want to like him but he was making it impossible not to. And as far as dealing with the kids went, she didn't have a better suggestion.

Every time CiCi thought she had Jake figured out, he did something unexpected. And then there was that kiss. Her reaction to that was embarrassing beyond words.

"Since I don't have another plan, I'm willing to give it a try," she said, hoping he couldn't tell where her mind had wandered. "What do you guys think?" She looked to the counselors for their input.

"It's worth a try," Greg said.

Chip merely nodded.

"Okay, let's do it."

"Are you *positive* you're okay with this idea?" Jake asked.

"Yeah. Let's do it." CiCi was right behind him when he marched into the dining room to confront Rondelle and his friends.

"Okay, guys, here's the deal—we're going to call this your second strike. That means if there's any more trouble, you're on your way back to Houston. You don't pass Go, you don't collect two hundred smackers, nothing. You're outta here."

Jake stared at each teen in turn, praying his words would have an effect. He looked to CiCi for confirmation.

"That's right," she said. "One more incident and you're toast."

Javier, Schulz, Timmy Smith and Shawn all turned to Rondelle for guidance. They were doing the teenage sheep routine that Jake remembered all too well.

Rondelle gave his co-conspirators a barely perceptible nod. "Okay, dude. You're the man. We won't get in no more trouble."

"Good. I'm going to hold you to it." Jake held his hand out for the unique handshake indigenous to the projects.

Rondelle nodded again and his friends lined up to shake hands.

Jake hoped he was giving them something they'd been missing, and that was trust. Too bad that was easier said than done.

Chapter Fourteen

A couple of days later Jake had just finished his morning workout when CiCi threw him a curveball. Camping? She wanted him to take forty kids camping? For two days? The only thing he knew about the great outdoors was what he'd learned at his ranch.

"I didn't exactly graduate from the Paul Bunyan school of Fine Camping."

"Oh, pooh. If I can do it, you can, too. Several of our counselors are majoring in outdoor activities. Besides, we won't be that far from civilization."

"Okay," Jake agreed. What choice did he have? She was his boss.

"Good. Now that that's settled, I have to talk to Cookie about our meals," she said with a cheeky grin. "If I had to cook, I'm afraid we'd all starve. The good news is that if you get too homesick for your bunk, you can always hitch a ride back to camp."

He wasn't likely to do that. Who knew, two days in a sleeping bag on the ground might be a welcome break from the horrible bed that threatened to cripple him every night. Where was that bed she'd promised?

CiCi WAS TRYING to appear confident, but when it came to camping, she was a neophyte. And to be perfectly honest she was a little surprised that he was as much of a newbie as she was.

She made herself put all thoughts of Jake aside when she met with the cook.

"I suggest we go with hot dogs, sandwiches, cereal, marsh-mallows, campfire kind of stuff," Cookie suggested. She'd been preparing meals at Camp Touchdown for years. "Nobody's gettin' sick on that."

"Sounds good to me." CiCi actually hadn't considered e-coli or salmonella. All she wanted was to make sure the kids were fed and happy, and if she could keep them occupied that would be a bonus.

The campground was five miles down the river—close enough to town for emergency services, but far enough away to make the kids feel as if they were having a wilderness adventure. In theory it sounded great but, it ended up being CiCi's personal idea of hell.

In fact, it made Miss Newcombe's Finishing School boot camp look like a walk in the park. She had so many mosquito bites she looked as if she had chicken pox. And yes, she'd used insect repellent. The damned things actually seemed to get off on the smell of the stuff.

And even worse, she had chigger bites in places too personal to mention. CiCi was tired, cranky and miserable, and that barely scratched the surface—no pun intended.

At the moment she was vainly trying to ignore a particularly annoying itch when a bloodcurdling scream made her blood pressure skyrocket. The noise was coming from over by the river. She prayed no one had drowned. Every staff member had a lifeguard certification, but accidents did happen. She barely made it ten feet before Jake raced by.

By the time CiCi reached the water's edge, a crowd had gathered. Horseshoes, badminton and even food were forgotten in the mad dash to find out what was happening.

At first glance it appeared that everything was okay. Jake wasn't pulling a dead body from the water and he wasn't doing CPR on anyone. So what was the fuss all about?

"What happened?" CiCi couldn't quite catch her breath.

"Shirley Lee saw a snake in the water." Jake's lip quivered with a barely suppressed grin. He had his arm around a lanky teen with cornrows, who was sniffling.

"Were any of the kids in the river?"

"A couple of them, but everyone's out now." Jake patted the girl on the back.

"Should we give up swimming for the day?" CiCi asked Bobby Ray, the head lifeguard. He was on the swim team at Baylor University, so he obviously knew his way around a pool, but perhaps a river was a different story.

"No need. Most of the water snakes around here are harmless. Besides, we've made so much noise that I'm sure everything wild has taken cover. They're more afraid of us than we are of them," he said.

That was a matter of opinion, but CiCi decided to put on a brave front. "Okay, let's make it optional. Anyone who doesn't want to swim can play volleyball or something." She waved her hand vaguely. That wasn't very decisive but it would have to do.

"I bet I couldn't pay you enough money to get in that water, could I?" Jake whispered close to her ear, sending goose bumps up and down her arms.

Call her a fool for letting her lust-o-meter run amok. She'd already had her share of heartbreak, thank you very much. All thoughts of Mr. Sexy had to be permanently banished.

Fat chance!

"Uh, probably not," she admitted with a self-deprecating laugh. "But I'm not about to admit that in front of the kids. I don't know what we'll do to entertain them if they won't go swimming."

"I see your point." Jake turned to the crowd of adolescents. "Last one in is a rotten egg!" he yelled, leading the charge into the shallow part of the water.

At times he seemed like a big kid. On other occasions, he was a philosopher and teen expert. She couldn't figure what made Jake Culpepper tick, but she also couldn't deny that she found him incredibly appealing.

The snake excitement died down, but the day and evening went on and on. Good God, CiCi felt as if she'd been banished to the wilderness for at least a century.

The calamine lotion had helped with the mosquito bites, but the chiggers were another story. Once they targeted you it was almost impossible to get rid of the itch—no matter how much lotion she applied.

"Are you having a good time?" Jake asked as he plopped down next to her at the river's edge. Sugar Plum immediately abandoned her mistress and put her head in his lap.

Stupid, fickle dog.

"I guess that depends on what you consider fun." CiCi covertly scratched an itchy spot.

"If you don't watch out those things will get infected, and from there you can get impetigo." He stretched out his long, tan legs. "I had impetigo when I was a kid. I couldn't go swimming for half the summer." Jake laughed. "That was probably one of my worst vacations ever."

"I've never heard of impetigo."

"I didn't think so. You have very beautiful skin." He ran a finger down her arm.

Although it was as hot as the tropics, his touch sent chills through her body.

"Um, thank you." That was probably the most inane comment she'd ever made, but she'd been out of the dating scene for a *very* long time. And more than likely his flirting was nothing more than a reflex.

"So…are you enjoying your time at the camp?"

Jake paused, apparently considering his answer. "Yeah, I think I am." He grinned sheepishly. "To tell the truth, I was really PO'd when Texas Bob sent me here. But as much as I hate to admit, I'm getting used to the kids. They take a lot of energy, don't they?"

"They certainly do. I'm glad it isn't as bad as you thought it would be. I was worried about working with you," she acknowledged. "But that's all changed. I really like you."

As far as compliments went, this one wasn't the most eloquent Jake had had. The significance of it, however, wasn't lost on him.

"I like you, too." To be totally honest, his feelings had moved closer to lust than like. Her lips were kissable, lush and soft, and that smooth olive skin was more tempting than he wanted to admit.

This shouldn't be happening. There were so many "don'ts" in this scenario that he'd have to be an idiot to kiss her. First of all, she was Texas Bob's daughter and that could be disastrous. Then they had about sixty nosy chaperones watching their every move, which in itself should be enough to tamp down any man's libido.

But disregarding their potential audience, Jake pulled CiCi into his arms. A moment later their lips met. He wasn't a novice at kissing; in fact, he'd had more than his share of experience. But kissing CiCi Hurst was an axis-altering, lightning-packed event. Their first kiss was nothing compared to this one.

His brain was telling him to breathe. His lips told him to keep kissing her. The peskiest voice of all was the doubt chiding him about the differences in their backgrounds.

But the truth was she wasn't anything like he'd initially expected. She was funny, warm, caring and too sexy for words.

He looked forward to hearing her laugh and watching her work with the campers. So he'd better watch out or he'd fall for Daddy's little princess and that would be a major-league blow to his career.

Jake was almost relieved when an adolescent squeal shocked them into pulling apart. Thanks to the twilight the kid probably hadn't seen anything.

"Hey, Coach, we've got a pickup volleyball game over by the campfire. Come be on our team." The request was made by Angel, his superstar, cheerleading kicker.

Fate had saved him from doing something incredibly stupid—like throwing CiCi Hurst to the ground and having his way with her.

"Sure," Jake agreed before turning his attention back to CiCi. He touched her bottom lip. "You're a big-time volleyball player. Do you want to make a friendly bet on the outcome?" He forced a grin that he didn't quite feel.

"Depends on what the bet is."

"If my team wins, I get another kiss," Jake whispered.

"What if my side wins?"

He shrugged, wondering what alien being had hijacked his mouth. That sucker was trying to get him in trouble. "It's your choice, as long as it involves kissing."

When she nodded and added a wink, Jake suspected he'd been had but couldn't see how she'd get out of it.

It was game point before Jake knew he'd truly been suckered. Angel was too short, Rondelle was too gangly, and Suarez was too hyper to even make it to the ball much less hit it back. That left Jake, and volleyball wasn't even close to his best game.

CiCi couldn't hide her gleeful grin as she spiked the winning point at his feet. His only consolation was that win, lose or draw, she'd agreed to a kiss. That made him a very lucky man.

At least that's what he thought right up until Sugar Plum presented her head for a big, slobbery kiss. They hadn't specified who would be doing the kissing.

CiCi Hurst was a wicked, wicked woman!

Chapter Fifteen

Had the camping trip really only lasted only two days? If so, that had to be the longest forty-eight hours in history.

While they were at the campsite the nurse had treated sunburn, insect bites and assorted bruises and contusions but kids were notoriously resilient. They didn't realize they should be uncomfortable and irritable.

CiCi was miserable enough for everyone, and she was desperate for a shower. But before she could indulge herself, she had to keep an eye on the kids as they unloaded their stuff. She was sitting on a picnic table examining a particularly nasty spot in the crook of her elbow when Jake joined her.

"Remember what I told you about impetigo."

She rolled her arm over for a better look. "Are you sure it's not a spider bite?"

Maybe she should just got up and go to the nurse—or then again, perhaps not.

"Let me check it out." He looked at her arm. "Nope, it's impetigo. I'd bet the farm on it." He delivered his diagnosis with a grin.

That smile should have a warning label. "Okay Dr. Culpepper, what do I do about it?"

"Antibiotic cream. Dwayne had impetigo so bad one time that he looked like a leper." Jake snorted. "We made him stay far away from us all summer. It wouldn't surprise me if he stole my Porsche to get back at me for making fun of him back then."

"How old *were* you?"

"Ten."

"Ten? You think he even remembers?"

"Oh, yeah." Jake's explanation was cut short by the arrival of the camp secretary, a young brunette named Kirsten.

"Miss CiCi, your dad called about an hour ago. He wanted me to tell you that they're on their way."

"My parents are coming here?"

"That's what they said." Kirsten gave Jake a flirty wave.

"How long do I have?"

"My guess is an hour, give or take." Kirsten jumped up on the table with Jake. "I'll keep an eye on things out here. That should give you time for a shower."

Jake also hadn't had a shower in two days. He should look like a bum, but he didn't, darn it.

CiCi glanced back and forth between Jake and Kirsten. Why hadn't Daddy hired some aging baby boomers? "I'll be back in ten minutes."

"Take your time," Jake answered.

What was he really saying? CiCi realized she needed some major renovation, but did he have to be snooty about it? Or was she just being touchy? Probably the latter.

JAKE WAS BUSY trying to discourage Kirsten when he heard a car horn blaring "The Eyes of Texas."

"Look at that!" the young woman squealed.

That was the longest vintage Cadillac Jake had ever seen. It was candy-apple red with a hood ornament straight off a Texas longhorn. The driver was none other than Texas Bob, and the woman riding shotgun was undoubtedly Mrs. Texas Bob.

When Jake leapt off the table, Kirsten sashayed back to

the office. Sugar Plum lumbered over to the car and stuck her head in the passenger window.

"Son, I sure hope you ain't been diddlin' the staff," Texas Bob said, climbing out of the Caddy. He huffed and puffed like the Texas version of *The Little Engine That Could*.

Jake knew that Winston Hurst had a degree from Harvard, and usually he thought it was funny when his boss turned into a tobacco chawin' redneck, but this time the good-old-boy act annoyed him.

"No, I'm not." Jake deliberately didn't add "sir" to the end of the sentence and stood as tall and straight as he could. Under normal circumstances, he didn't use his size to intimidate, but right now it seemed appropriate. And much to his surprise, it worked.

"Don't get your boxers in a bunch, son. I apologize. My wife tells me I'm bad about jumping to conclusions."

"Winston, your mother taught you better manners than that." Mrs. Texas Bob *tsked* at her husband before turning to Jake. "Hi, Jake. I don't know if you remember me, I'm Marianne Hurst," she said, extending her hand. "We met at a symphony fund-raiser."

"Yes, ma'am, I haven't forgotten." Actually he had, but if there was ever a time for a white lie, this was it.

"Hi, Jake." Mac waved at him while trying to keep Sugar Plum from giving her daughter a bath of doggie kisses. "Remember me?"

"Sure. How are you doing?" He hadn't noticed CiCi's sister and niece until they emerged from the backseat.

Mac lifted a finger to ask him to wait. "Molly!" she said. "Go run with Sugar Plum. And stay on the grass."

Molly responded by doing a series of cartwheels across the lawn. Sugar Plum chased after her, obviously thrilled to have a new playmate.

"She just started gymnastics. We can't seem to keep her still."

Jake was impressed by the way Mac could multitask, conducting an intelligent conversation without taking her eyes off her daughter.

"Where's CiCi?" Marianne asked.

"She's taking a shower. We just got back from a two-day camping trip, so we're a little ripe. Why don't you go on inside where it's cool? I'll wander back to the kitchen and see if I can rustle up some drinks."

"That's very nice of you. Come on, Winston." She grabbed her husband's arm, steering him toward the lodge.

"I'll join you in a minute," Mac said as she made herself at home in one of the twig rockers to watch Molly play with the dog.

Jake had a vision of petite blonde Marianne Hurst dragging Texas Bob along by the ear. It was good to know that someone could get the best of the ultimate BS expert.

CICI HAD NEVER taken such a quick shower. She didn't want Daddy to hear about the shenanigans at the camp. She'd had enough failures, both professional and personal, to last a lifetime, and she certainly wasn't anxious to add this one to the list.

She didn't bother putting on makeup or drying her hair before she ran down the stairs of the main lodge. Too late. Mama and Daddy were having lemonade with Jake as if they were old friends.

Mama would die if she thought her daughter had the hots for another playboy athlete. CiCi would have to be permanently on guard so she didn't give anything away.

"Hi, Mama. Hi, Daddy. I didn't expect to see you guys."

"We decided to drive up and see how you're doing," her

mother answered. "And did you lose something while you were out camping?"

CiCi poured herself a glass of lemonade. "Like what?"

"Like your manners. How about a hug?"

"Oops. Sorry. I'm a little frazzled." She wrapped her arms around her mom.

"Have you gone to the nurse about that impetigo?"

If one more person asked her about her "oowie" she was going to scream. "No, but I will."

It looked as if Jake was trying to keep from laughing. He probably thought the Hursts were all entertaining, but at least Daddy was the only family member who had a pair of horns affixed to the hood of his car.

"So," CiCi said after finishing off half a glass of lemonade in one gulp. "How long are you staying?"

Mama gave her the dreaded raised eyebrow.

"A day, maybe two," Daddy answered. "I had some business in San Antonio, so we thought we'd run up for a little visit. Aren't you glad to see your folks?"

CiCi knew when to give in. "Of course I'm glad you're here." She gave her dad a squeeze. "I'm just exhausted from communing with Mother Nature. I'm afraid I'm not much of a pioneer. So, I'll introduce you to the campers while Jake takes a shower. Then we can all have lunch. How about that?"

"Sounds good." Texas Bob grinned. "Yep, that sounds mighty good. Let's go round up Molly and Mac."

"Molly and Mac are here?"

"Molly is off somewhere with Sugar Plum, but Mac's on the front porch." Marianne gave CiCi a wink. "When your sister heard we were coming, she hitched a ride. You know how nosy she can be."

CiCi heard only a portion of what her mother was saying as she rushed out the door.

"Mac." She had missed her sister like crazy even if she did

think Cole Benavides was a mistake. "Why didn't you tell me you were coming?" She pulled Mac into a hug.

"I didn't want to give you time to make up some silly story. Enquiring minds want to know. We're having a slumber party tonight." Mac gave CiCi a saucy hip butt. "I want the straight skinny, all of it."

Perhaps a heart-to-heart was exactly what CiCi needed, either that or a lobotomy. Jake's kiss had been a scorcher, but did it mean anything to him? She still couldn't get past the fact that he was a jock and a groupie magnet.

"That sounds perfect, but what about Molly?"

"She's bunking with Mom and Dad in the guestroom. You're going to have to share your bed with me—unless it's already too crowded," Mac said with a suggestive wink.

"I only wish." Or did she? Could she take a chance on a man again and not get her heart broken? And when had she turned into such a chicken? That was easy—it happened when Jake Culpepper mistook her for a mutant fowl.

Chapter Sixteen

Although Marianne and Texas Bob were intimately familiar with the camp, they dutifully "oohed" and "aahed" during the guided tour.

"Where is everyone?" Marianne asked as they walked back from the ball fields. "I thought the kids would be out, playing."

CiCi suspected most of them were napping. A couple of nights in the great outdoors would zap the Energizer Bunny.

"I think everyone has gone to their cabins for a little snooze."

Marianne nodded. "That makes sense."

"So, Dad, what do you think?"

"Sweetheart, you're doing a great job, really terrific." Texas Bob gave her another hug. "Tell you what, though. I wouldn't mind cutting the tour short and heading back for some chow. I'm starved. Do you think we could eat before the feeding frenzy starts?"

CiCi twined her arm through his. "You may have to make do with tuna sandwiches. We haven't replenished our supplies."

"I don't like fish sandwiches," Molly said as she skipped up with Mac right behind her.

CiCi ruffled her niece's curls. "PB&J for you."

"With potato chips?"

"Absolutely. And a Sprite if that's okay with your mom."

Mac grinned. "I don't like fish sandwiches, either."

"You girls just don't know what's good. I'm sure anything Cookie prepares will be delicious." Marianne marched straight to the kitchen when they reached the lodge, ready to help if necessary.

The day went amazingly well. Daddy was pleased with how smoothly things were operating, and Jake had been charming. What more could she want? That was easy—a soft bed and a good night's rest.

BUT THAT WASN'T in the cards, especially since she was sharing her bed with Chatty Kathy.

"I want to hear everything," Mac demanded. Her position, seated in the middle of the bed with a bowl of popcorn in her lap, made her look more like a teenager than a divorced single mom.

CiCi flopped back against the headboard. The scene reminded her a lot of high school. "There's not much to tell. He kissed me. That's it."

"That's it? What do you mean?" Mac had devoured the popcorn and was now working on a two-pound bag of mini Milky Ways.

"Sometimes I think he's attracted to me." CiCi smiled thinking about those steamy kisses. "Especially when we... you know."

"Duh! Of course he's hot for you." Mac wasn't known for her patience. "You're a beautiful woman. Who wouldn't be?"

"Remember Tank. I didn't exactly walk away from that with my self-esteem intact."

Mac waved her hand in dismissal. "He's an idiot—what does he know?"

Tank *was* a moron. But CiCi wasn't in the mood to talk about him. "So, what's going on with you and Cole Benavides?" How was that for a slick segue?

Mac managed to look both a chagrined and happy. "We've met at Starbucks a couple of times, that's all." She shrugged eloquently. "A latte at ten o'clock in the morning isn't exactly a date, is it?"

"Beats me. I wouldn't recognize a real date if it smacked me in the face. We're pretty pitiful, aren't we?"

"Yep," Mac agreed. "You'd think we would've learned our lesson about men, especially the ones who can't seem to keep their pants up. But I think—I hope—that Cole is different."

CiCi realized she was playing with fire even thinking about getting involved with Jake, but whether it was lunacy, dementia or self-delusion, she couldn't help herself.

"Let's discuss this logically." In the two years since her divorce CiCi hadn't allowed herself to talk about her feelings. Mama wanted her to go to a therapist, but she'd resisted.

"Intellectually I think that I did everything I could to make a good marriage. But in my heart—" she thumped her chest "—I'm not quite sure."

Mac scrunched up her face. The expression was so reminiscent of their childhood that CiCi laughed, even if the subject wasn't funny.

"Join the crowd." Mac leaned over to put the bag of candy on the nightstand. "When I was a football wife, I'd hear about some guy having an affair and think it was terrible. In my naïveté I assumed it would never happen to me." She sighed.

"I suppose I thought that if I worked out and took care of myself, everything would be fine. But there's always someone skinnier or prettier out there, and if the guy you're with doesn't have a moral compass… Well, we both know what happens."

Wasn't that the truth!

"I knew it wasn't my fault," Mac continued. "I still don't know what he was looking for, and frankly I don't care. My job now is to make a happy life for me and Molly."

CiCi admired her sister's spunk. "So you don't think all this crap happened because we married athletes?"

"Maybe, maybe not. I think the problem was more that they had countless women falling at their feet."

"Yeah," CiCi agreed. This conversation was depressing. "Do you think you might get serious about Cole?"

"I don't know. I'm going to wait and see. I'm hesitant to do anything, but that doesn't mean I'm giving up on life, and neither should you."

"I'm trying. And," CiCi said with a giggle, "my dilemma now is whether I should start with Jake Culpepper, Mr. Date Every Good Looking Blonde with a D-cup, or go for someone safer."

"Here, have some chocolate. You might need it when you hear what I'm about to tell you." Mac tossed her a couple of Milky Ways. "Do you know someone named Brenda Olson?"

"No. Why?" CiCi was getting a bad vibe from her sister's sober tone.

"There's no easy way to say this, but yesterday in the About Town column in the paper there was an article about her." Mac paused.

"So what?" CiCi asked. Why should she care what the paper wrote about someone she'd never heard of?

"She's apparently announced that she's engaged to Jake Culpepper."

"Crap!" CiCi felt as though someone had just punched her in the stomach.

"Here, take the chocolate." Mac handed over the bag. "I think you need it more than I do."

JAKE WOKE UP the next morning with a sense of dread. CiCi had asked him to entertain her dad. Spending the day with Texas Bob was about the last thing he wanted to do, but hey—

So on that note he tied his shoes and strolled to the cafeteria for breakfast.

Jake was enjoying his second cup of coffee, and congratulating himself on avoiding his boss when he heard that unmistakable booming voice.

"I hear you're doin' a good job here," Texas Bob said as he sat down at Jake's table.

"I hope so. The kids seem to be enjoying themselves."

"I also hear you guys have been having trouble with a few of the kids." Texas Bob stirred a heaping spoonful of sugar into his coffee.

Jake wondered what CiCi had told her father and how much he should divulge. "We had a couple of problems but I think we handled them fairly well."

"Yeah, that's what CiCi said, too." Texas Bob was gazing into his coffee as if he was trying to read the grounds. Didn't that only worked on tea? "What do you think of my daughter?"

That question was unexpected. "We have a great working relationship." Jake wasn't about to volunteer anything more, especially to CiCi's dad.

"My daughter would kill me if she knew I told you this, but here goes. She's very vulnerable right now and I'd hate like hell to see her hurt."

Jake took a deep breath. This was not the time to lose his temper. "I don't intend to hurt her."

"I read that article about Brenda Olson." Texas Bob paused as if he expected a comment.

"What article?" Jake knew for sure he wouldn't like whatever came next. Brenda had caused him nothing but trouble.

"She's saying that you two are engaged."

"What!"

"Is it true?"

"Absolutely not!"

Texas Bob ran his fingers through his hair. "Okay, I'll take your word for it. Let's go watch some kids play ball."

It was amazing how he could switch subject on a dime, but in this case it suited Jake just fine. He had some thinking to do.

By early afternoon Daddy was packing the car getting ready to leave. "Are you sure you have to go home?" CiCi asked her mom.

"Yes, honey," Marianne answered. "Not that we don't want to spend time with you, but Mac has to get back to work and I have an important meeting tomorrow." She hoisted her purse on her shoulder before she took CiCi's hand. "For what it's worth, and I can't believe I'm saying this, but I really like Jake."

Had CiCi given off some vibe that Mama had picked up on? "He's a nice guy and a great addition to the staff, but otherwise, I'm not sure I see your point."

"Collier, please, I'm your *mother*." Marianne waved a hand in obvious dismissal. "Keep an open mind but be careful. You know there are some rumors floating around about him."

"I know. Mac told me about the article in the paper."

"Your daddy talked to Cole and he claims this woman's not stable. And Jake apparently also says she's lying. He's probably telling the truth, but it wouldn't hurt to be cautious. Having said that, I think it's high time you came back to the land of the living, and I'm not talking about your professional life." She gave CiCi a hug. "We'll discuss this more when you get home."

CiCi certainly looked forward to *that* conversation. "Don't worry about me. I'm fine. Really, I am."

"No, you're not. You're marching in place. All I'm saying is that if you're interested in Mr. Culpepper, you have our blessing. And believe me, that wasn't an easy sell with your dad."

Daddy would probably think of his daughters as his baby girls until they were eligible for Social Security.

CiCi gave her mother another hug. "We didn't get much chance to visit, but I'm glad you came."

"I am, too."

"Hop in the car, snookums." That was Daddy's pet name for Marianne. "Where did Mac and Molly run off to?"

"They're over there." Marianne indicated Molly, who was playing with Sugar Plum and Mac, who was trying to herd her daughter to the car.

"Come on, girls, let's go!" Daddy yelled, then turned to CiCi.

"We need to get going before it starts to rain. I heard on the radio that we're in for some nasty stuff. Check out what's happening up to the northwest." Texas Bob indicated the sky over his left shoulder.

"Oh, my word," Marianne said. "We'd better hit the road or we're going to get caught in a frog strangler."

CiCi was slightly concerned. Summer storms were usually light-and-sound shows accompanied by heavy rain. But since the Texas Hill Country was notorious for flash flooding, and the camp was located right on the river, that could be a problem. "Did they say we're under a tornado watch?"

"They didn't say anything about tornados," Daddy said. "I hate to leave you but I think we'll try to outrun the storm. If you have any more trouble with the kids, call me."

"We'll be fine," CiCi assured him, not quite convinced she was telling the truth.

"Okay." Texas Bob hugged his daughter one last time before he helped his wife into the car.

Molly jumped into the backseat but Mac hung back a few seconds. "Call me tomorrow." She made the sign of a phone with her thumb and little finger.

Sugar Plum tried to shove her way into the backseat with them. "You're staying here." Mac pushed on the big dog's head. "Grab her collar, CiCi. I love her, but I don't want to share my seat with her all the way to Houston."

CiCi couldn't fault that logic. "Come here, sweetie." Sugar Plum gave a big woof but reluctantly complied. It almost looked as if the dog was trying to wave.

Mac got Molly strapped into her car seat before rolling down the back window. "You be careful, now, ya hear? Love you." She and Molly both threw kisses.

"If the weather gets bad, pull over and wait it out," CiCi yelled as her daddy threw the car in gear. He waved, indicating he'd heard her.

Chapter Seventeen

CiCi and Jake watched as the dust the Caddy kicked up slowly settled. "He's not going to listen, you know that, don't you?" Jake said.

"Yeah, I do."

He rubbed her neck, loosening the knots in her muscles. It had been a long week and a half.

"That feels good." In fact, it was so nice she could have purred.

"I almost hate to say this but I enjoyed your parents. I didn't see much of your mom, but I had an interesting talk with your dad. He's nothing like I thought he was."

"Apparently the feeling was mutual. They liked you, too," CiCi said and then abruptly changed the subject. "Did you hear the weather forecast? Daddy told me the weather service is predicting a bad rainstorm."

"I haven't been listening to the radio. What about tornadoes?"

"He didn't think so. But look at that." She pointed toward the northwest where devilishly dark clouds were swirling like fudge boiling in a pot. "We could be in for some *really* bad stuff."

"Crap! Do we have a storm shelter and a weather alert radio?"

"No to the cellar, yes to the radio." Jake was normally cool, calm and collected, but the way he was examining the sky raised her panic level a notch.

"I think we'd better get everyone into the lodge. I'll ring the emergency gong."

Before CiCi could say a word, Jake was off and running. The campers knew that if the gong sounded, they were supposed to head immediately to the main building.

Texas weather was unpredictable, at best. Folks on the coast dealt with hurricanes, tropical storms, torrential rains and an occasional drought. In the Panhandle, residents were familiar with funnel clouds, ice storms, blizzards and gully washers. In El Paso country, they'd go for months without a drop of rain and then without warning the remnants of a Pacific hurricane would roar through and they'd have flash floods. Unfortunately, the Hill Country got a little of everything.

By the time the last camper made it to the lodge, the god of thunder was putting on a show that could rival a Fourth of July celebration and the rain was sheeting down.

"Are we above the flood plain?" Jake asked as he stared out the window.

"The water's never gotten this high so we should be all right here," CiCi said. "I don't know what'll happen with the rest of the property. The last time we had a flood we had to rebuild all the sports fields."

The news on the radio wasn't optimistic. The front had stalled over central Texas and the storm was expected to last another three to four hours and to produce at least ten inches of rain. That definitely meant flooding.

"At least we're safe. I'm not sure our sanity will hold up," Jake joked, referring to the noise created by forty kids in an enclosed space. Cookie had provided snacks, and the staff members were trying to keep everyone interested in games, but it wasn't working. "It's kind of loud, isn't it?" he yelled.

"It certainly is."

"Coach!" Rondelle called from across the room. "Come join us in a foosball game." Rondelle and Timmy Smith were arguing over which team he would join.

"Looks like I've been summoned." Jake smiled at CiCi before strolling over to the combatants. "Comin'."

CiCi watched her favorite tight end saunter off. Even, or maybe especially, from the rear, that was a sight to behold. Not only was he good-looking enough to entice almost any female, he was a nice guy. Why couldn't he be a pain?

With that thought in mind, CiCi mentally prepared to endure the storm without killing the teenage captives.

Three hours later, the rain had slowed to a drizzle and the fierce wind was nothing more than a memory.

"I think we can release the prisoners." Jake stood at the window, watching the remnants of the storm. He was close enough to raise goose bumps up and down her neck.

"Before we do that, I'd like you to come with me to inspect the grounds." When it came to the kids' safety she wasn't going to take any chances. "When the river rises, the snakes look for high ground."

"What you plan to do if we find one?"

"We'll play it by ear." That was a euphemism for "I don't have a clue." "Sugar Plum, you stay here." That silly dog would probably jump in the water and they'd never see her again. "And, Greg, keep the kids inside until we get back."

"Right, boss," the counselor responded.

"Come on, big guy," she said to Jake. Although he wasn't enthusiastic, he did follow her outside.

They surveyed the grounds for damage. The cabins were fine. And although several tree limbs had been blown down by the high wind and water was running in rivulets through the grass, the overall destruction was minimal.

Jake was looking around as if expecting something to jump

out and grab him. "I don't see any snakes. What do you want to do now?"

The big, bad football player was afraid of snakes? How about that! "Don't tell me you're scared of a couple of cottonmouths."

"Damn straight," he admitted.

CiCi had to give him points for honesty, but back to business. She pulled out her cell phone and punched in Greg's number.

"You can let the inmates go, but be sure to tell them to stay near the lodge. And please organize some of the staff into a cleaning crew."

"You got it," he said, before disconnecting.

"Greg will get things going up there, so let's wander down to the river and see how bad it is."

They soon discovered that while the camp had been spared, the river was another story. Toppled trees and debris from outbuildings bobbed and weaved as the water raced toward the Gulf of Mexico.

Although most of the wreckage would be caught by a mammoth dam downstream, that was no consolation to the folks who had lost everything.

"There's a car." CiCi pointed at a small vehicle that was momentarily caught on something in the middle of the river. Then, in the blink of an eye, it was gone. "Do you think there was anyone in it?" She was trying to be calm, but not having much success.

"I couldn't tell for sure. I didn't see anyone, but that doesn't mean much."

"Coach! Coach!" CiCi was surprised to see Rondelle sprinting toward them. His normal chocolate color was blanched pale. What had happened to the "stay by the lodge" instruction?

Jake grabbed the kid's arm. "What's going on?"

"It's Angel." Rondelle bent over and retched.

"What about her?"

"She slipped into the river!"

"Good God!" CiCi was afraid she was going to lose it. That child could die and it was all her fault.

Jake put his hands on her shoulders and gave her a gentle shake.

"Call 911 and tell them to get over here ASAP." He turned back to Rondelle. "Show me where she went in." A second later he was running down the riverbank with the teen.

CiCi immediately made the call, but the news wasn't good. A church bus had been washed off the road several miles upstream and there were dozens of kids stranded in the trees. According to the sheriff's office every emergency responder in that part of the county was working on rescuing them. It would be at least fifteen to twenty minutes before anyone could get to Camp Touchdown. By that time CiCi knew Angel could very well be gone. They were on their own.

CiCi ran to the ridge where Jake and Rondelle were surveying the water. The dock had been swept away by the normally languid river that had become a deadly torrent of swirling water.

"Bloody hell!" Jake exclaimed after CiCi gave him the update. He was frantically scanning the river, trying to catch sight of the girl. "We can't wait twenty minutes. As fast as that water's running she could be in New Braunfels by then."

"I see her! She's down there!" CiCi pointed toward a clump of trees that only yesterday had been on dry ground, but was now surrounded by an eddy of brown water. Angel's golden hair had caught CiCi's attention, and she realized the child was clinging to a tree branch. They had to get her out of there right away.

Jake took one look and without a word, raced down the slight incline. CiCi tripped and slid trying to keep up with him.

"God, what a mess!" Jake put both hands on his head. "I'm going to have to go out there and get her." He motioned for CiCi to remain where she was while he moved closer to the raging water.

She was supposed to stay high and dry while he risked his life? No way! All of a sudden she had an idea.

"Don't do anything until I get back," CiCi shouted to be heard over the roar of the river. "Rondelle, come with me," she told the teen. "We're going to get some life jackets and a rope. Don't move a muscle, 'ya hear!"

"Yes, ma'am," Jake replied with a mock salute.

THERE WAS SO MUCH DEBRIS swirling around Angel that Jake was shocked she could hold on. And there was no telling how long that would last. He did a quick estimate of the distance between the bank and the tree. It was no more than ten feet and normally that wouldn't be a problem. In these conditions, it was an abyss.

Jake's brain was going a mile a minute, trying to come up with a plan, when CiCi returned, carrying a bright orange ski vest and several life preservers. Rondelle was right behind her with a coil of rope looped over his shoulder.

"Don't come down here—it's too dangerous." Jake didn't want CiCi that close to the water, but he sure could use the group of burly counselors she had with her. Thank God the cavalry had arrived.

"Oh, all right," she conceded.

"You guys be careful getting down!" Jake yelled, the noise of the water almost drowning him out. "It's slick. And, Greg, Keep the kids up on the top of the hill, especially Rondelle." His favorite juvie was the most likely to try something silly, and the last thing they needed was someone else in the drink. Jake grabbed the ski vest CiCi tossed him and slipped it on.

Heaven help them, they were on their own. Whatever they did, they'd better do it pretty damned quick.

Jake called the college kids over and told them his idea. "I'm going to tie a rope around my waist and jump in upstream. Then I'm going to try to swim to the tree. And after I get Angel tied to me, you guys pull like mad. I'm counting on you." He was hoping like hell he wasn't too heavy for this plan to work. These young men were literally his lifeline in this skirmish with the river. If they let go, he and Angel were both in a ton of trouble.

Chapter Eighteen

This was officially the most terrifying day of CiCi's life. Was Jake really going to jump into the river roiling with debris, and snakes and who knew what else? It would be a miracle if he made it out alive. *Please, God. Please, God. Please, God!*

CiCi muttered the prayer over and over. She didn't notice when Greg had joined her.

"I just thought you'd want to know. The kids are all okay," he said. "A couple of the boys are hot to come down and help. But don't worry, my crew has everything under control. And I've stationed someone at the front gate to show the emergency folks where we are when they get here."

CiCi couldn't keep her eyes off the activity at the water's edge. "Good. We don't need anyone else getting hurt."

"Do you want to go down there and see if we can help?" Greg asked, referring to the area where Jake and the counselors were mounting the rescue effort.

"Jake's going to have a fit, but yeah, let's go. But first let's put these on." CiCi handed Greg one of the extra life preservers.

"Good idea," he said as he slipped into the orange vest. "Let me go in front. Maybe I can stop us if we start to fall." Greg grabbed a branch and took one step and then another.

CiCi didn't think she was a coward, but his suggestion did make sense. "Okay."

A slip, a slide and a few heart-stopping moments later, they made it to the riverbank. She was breathing hard but that was probably from sheer terror.

The counselors were lined up as if they were participating in a game of tug-of-war, but this time winning was a matter of life or death.

"I'm going to help them." Greg started to walk away but CiCi stopped him.

"Do you think he's strong enough to swim out there?" Not many people were as big as Jake Culpepper but pitted against an out-of-control river, that didn't mean much.

"If anyone can do it, he can."

CiCi wasn't sure that was the answer she wanted, but it would have to do.

Jake's first attempt missed. The guys pulled and slid and cussed until they finally retrieved him. CiCi's knees were about to buckle, she felt light-headed and, even worse, she was afraid she was going to lose her lunch—and she wasn't the one risking her life.

Thirty minutes—and a couple of terrifying misses—later, Jake and Angel were safely on the shore. Although they were both covered in scrapes and bruises, they were alive.

Alive! Thank God!

THE MINUTE Jake touched dry land he decided to never underestimate the power of water again. He was a strong guy, but still there had been several times he'd thought he was a goner. He was tempted to drop to his knees and kiss the ground.

Fifteen minutes later, the sheriff and a fire truck arrived in an impressive display of lights and sirens. They were a day late and a dollar short, but at least the emergency medical technicians could check out Angel. When it came to the physical well-being of someone that small and fragile Jake was out of his element.

Whap, whap, whap. That was the unmistakable sound of a helicopter.

"Why are they here?" CiCi pointed at the sky and yelled to be heard over the noise.

"I suspect we're about to get a visit from a San Antonio TV crew," the sheriff answered. "They were here for the bus accident and it went out over the scanner that Jake Culpepper was involved in a rescue, so..." The lawman didn't need to finish his sentence.

Great! It hadn't taken long for the news to spread. Jake was still trying to catch his breath when one of the choppers landed and an opportunistic reporter with his cameraman hopped out.

"Hey, we heard that you're a hero!" the man yelled. Jake didn't have time to respond before a camera was stuck in his face.

"What are you doing in the Hill Country?"

Jake thought a second before answering, trying to come up with the most innocuous explanation possible. "I'm a volunteer at the camp, and now I have things to do, like get into some dry clothes. I'm sure you understand. Come visit me when we're having the Road Runners' training camp. I'll give you an interview then." By that time, several other reporters had arrived, lured by the news that Jake Culpepper had been involved in a rescue.

He'd had plenty of experience dealing with the media so he was able to extricate himself with a small measure of grace. Or at least he thought he had.

"Look, I'm fine," Jake assured the emergency medical technician who had insisted on checking him out.

"I'm sure you are." That didn't stop the man from taking his blood pressure—again. "So how do you think the Road Runners will do this year?"

Ah, that was it. Jake's brain must be full of water, or mush, not to immediately figure out what was going on. If he didn't watch out, he'd end up signing autographs.

Football in Texas was king, and the men who played it, from high school kids to college stars to Pro Bowlers, were the crown princes.

"I'm through here." The technician stowed his blood pressure cuff. "Would you autograph this?" He tore a piece of paper out of a notebook and handed it to Jake. "It's for my kid."

He'd sure called that one right.

CiCi's FIRST JOB WAS to check on Angel. The teen had some scraped and abrasions, but other than that she was fine—and that was all thanks to Jake. The man would never admit it, but he was a hero.

And speaking of the hero, he was surrounded by a crowd of men who, from the looks of things, all wanted an autograph. Oh, boy, fame had to be quite a pain in the butt.

Maybe this time Jake would appreciate being rescued himself. "Hey, guys, would you all like to come to the dining room for a cup of coffee?" she called.

"Sure!" A sheriff's deputy was the first to answer, but there were nods all around.

THE NOISE LEVEL in the dining hall was only marginally lower than a rock concert. But what would you expect after that kind of adrenaline rush?

"Hey, Greg." Despite the pandemonium, CiCi managed to get his attention. "These folks would like to get Jake's autograph. Could you please keep the kids occupied?"

"Sure. Hey, you guys," Greg yelled to his staff. "Drag out the boom box. We need to lighten up, so we're going to have a dance."

"Let's go back to the kitchen," CiCi suggested to the autograph seekers. "In about five minutes we won't be able to hear ourselves think."

Jake made his way through the kids like a modern-day Moses striding through the Red Sea. They'd almost made it to the kitchen door before the music started.

Bumpety bumpety bump! It was so loud CiCi could feel the bass thumping through her shoes. There were kids everywhere—rocking, grinding and generally turning themselves into contortionists. Rondelle was poppin' with a couple of his buddies. A crowd of admirers had formed around Angel. She had bumps and bruises, but according to the medics she was going to be okay.

"That's better," Jake said as he closed the door to the kitchen. "At least we can talk."

"Are they always that…enthusiastic?" the sheriff asked.

It appeared that even John Law wasn't immune to football fever. Hopefully, this little autograph session would go a long way toward building a good rapport with the local constabulary—something they might need later if any of the campers crossed the line again.

"Most of the time," CiCi admitted. "But they're good kids."

Chapter Nineteen

A couple of days after the storm Jake and the counselors were clearing debris from the natural swimming hole. Just looking at him was enough to send CiCi into cardiac arrest. He was stripped down to nothing more than a pair of cargo shorts, a straw cowboy hat and running shoes, and man oh man, that bod was impressive. Broad shoulders, massive biceps and that chest—well, it was…it was…tanned and buff and, good God!

Cease and desist! She needed more than a good body. Tank had one, but that didn't stop him from being a worm.

"Jake!" Oops, that sounded snippy. When he glanced up, she softened her tone. "May I talk to you for a sec?"

"Sure." Jake wiped the sweat off his face with his discarded T-shirt. "We're almost finished." He turned to his coworkers. "Can you do without me for little bit?"

"Sure," answered the burliest of the three counselors. Texas Bob hadn't hired any pencil-necked geeks.

"This humidity is hell." Jake pulled his T-shirt over his head.

Why had he covered such a nice view?

"What do you think?" He indicated the work they'd done on the swimming hole.

CiCi had been so immersed in her prurient fantasies that

she hadn't noticed. It took a mental slap to get her back on track. "It's fantastic. The kids will be thrilled."

Blue Hole was a spring-fed swimming hole that was a favorite with the campers. And considering CiCi was a big fan of keeping hormonal teens well-fed and entertained, she was thrilled with the result.

"Thanks, guys," she said, expressing her appreciation to the crew of workers.

"So, what can I do for you?" Jake dropped down on a tree stump, wiping his face again with the hem of his shirt. "Want one?" he asked, reaching into a cooler for a bottle of Gatorade.

"No, thanks."

"Okay," he said, taking a big swallow.

How did he make drinking an energy drink look sexy?

"So what did you want to talk to me about?"

What *did* she want to talk to him about? Oh, yeah. "I just wanted to pick your brain about how to keep the kids busy with something they enjoy so they don't have time to think up any more shenanigans. I don't think I can take any more of this angst."

There was so much riding on her success with Camp Touchdown—her pride, her self-esteem and last but certainly not least, Daddy's approval.

"I've been thinking about that," Jake began, but before he could continue they were interrupted.

"Coach, Miz Hurst!" Javier, Rondelle's buddy, came running up out of breath. "There's somthin' bad goin' down at the main lodge. You'd better come quick!"

Jake frowned but didn't say a word before he sprinted across the lawn. CiCi was right behind him.

What the heck was going on? Rondelle was sitting on a stringy-haired man in a cheap suit while Schwartz and a couple of other kids stood guard, armed with sticks.

Heaven help her!

"You." CiCi pointed at the intruder. "Get up and tell me what you're doing here. I won't tolerate violence. It's not good for the kids."

She ignored the "are you kidding?" look Jake gave her. He was probably thinking juvie records, car theft, shoplifting and now assault.

"Get. Up!" she repeated when the man stayed down even after Rondelle released him.

The refugee from Sleazy 'R' Us was writhing on the ground with his hands plastered on his head.

"Keep…them…away…from me."

"Coach. Coach!" Rondelle was trying to get Jake's attention. "He was crawling around in the bushes with a big camera. It looked as if he was trying to get close enough to take a picture of you. I think he's one of those papa sans."

"A papa san?"

"I think he means a paparazzi," CiCi guessed.

"A paparazzi?" Jake squatted to get eyeball-to-eyeball with the intruder. "Hey, man, what's this all about?"

The man moaned.

What a dweeb, CiCi thought. "You're a trespasser and I'm calling the cops." She yanked the cell phone out of her pocket.

"Don't do that." The photographer got on his knees and waved a hand in Jake's direction. "He's a hot commodity, big-time hot. Getting an interview would make my career."

"Not your call, buddy." This guy had tabloid reporter written all over him. Knowing how newsworthy Jake was, she should've seen this coming.

"I'm goin', I'm goin'." He jumped up and ran to the front gate. The next thing they heard was an engine firing up.

"I wonder how long he's been slinking around here." CiCi

also wondered whether the trespasser had seen Jake kissing her the night of Angel's rescue. She'd been distraught and he'd been comforting.

Chapter Twenty

Two days later, while Jake was still pondering his paparazzi encounter, more trouble came a'calling in the form of Cousin Dwayne. That man was a true idiot. Not only was he driving Jake's Porsche—which had made it through auto rehab—he was accompanied by none other than Brenda Olson. How had he gotten that car key?

No doubt about it, Dwayne was roadkill.

Brenda spotted him almost immediately. She jumped out of the sports car and launched herself at him—arms around his neck, legs wrapped around his waist. Unfortunately, Jake's brain didn't engage fast enough to block her.

Oblivious to their growing audience, Brenda rained kisses all over his face. Jake was trying to disentangle himself when he spied CiCi watching them. If looks could kill he'd be six feet under.

"Jake, Jake," Brenda whined. "We need to talk. Really, honey, we do."

Prying her off was like pulling bubble gum from a hot sidewalk, but Jake was determined. "Please get your hands and your body off me."

"Aw, Jake. We could—"

"No, we couldn't. Let go. I mean it!"

Brenda demonstrated a pout worthy of Paris Hilton but

dropped to the ground. "I just wanted to congratulate you on being so famous."

"Famous? What are you talking about?"

She looked at him as though he'd just lost his mind. "You've had millions of hits on your YouTube video. Everyone in Houston thinks you're a hero. In fact, I heard a rumor that *People* magazine wants to do a spread on you, or was that the *National Enquirer?*" She propped her chin up with a manicured nail to signal how hard she was thinking.

"A video of what?"

"You silly man." Brenda poked that same finger at his chest. "It's a film of you rescuing that girl." She pointed out Angel in the crowd of teens. "It's quite the hit."

Jake glanced at Brenda and then Angel. Obviously someone had filmed that near disaster and then put it on the Internet. It wouldn't have been his first choice, but with his contract coming up for renewal, some good publicity might be useful—but maybe not.

CiCi HAD BEEN on the porch of the lodge contemplating the past three weeks when the sleek black Porsche rocketed up the gravel drive and crunched to a stop. She took one look at the blonde's big hair, Miss America body and toothpaste-white smile, and her heart sank like the *Titanic*. She couldn't compete with that.

Wait a minute! Her insecurities were showing, and dammit, she wasn't going to let them rule her life.

CiCi was too chicken to get close enough to hear what was happening so she was trying to read Jake's expressions. At first, he looked as though steam was about to pour out of his ears. And when the bimbo wrapped around herself around him like Saran Wrap, he seemed embarrassed. But the more they talked, the more baffled he appeared.

So what *was* going on?

THE MOMENT Jake processed what Brenda had told him, he steered his cousin toward the Porsche. "It's time for you guys to leave. It's late and I don't want you driving my car after dark." He didn't yell, but his cousin got the message.

Dwayne put his hands up in the classic signal of surrender. "Hey, man. Don't get in a dither. I thought I'd run up and let you know your car's as good as new. And Brenda wanted to come say hi, so here we are."

Jake opened the car door and pushed him in. "That was a very bad idea. When you get back to Houston leave my car at my condo and give the keys to the concierge. Do not go near any of my other vehicles. Don't call me, don't call my mother and don't contact Aunt Pallie. When I want to talk to you, I'll let you know. If I hear even a peep that you've been driving this car again I'll report it stolen and let the cops take care of you."

After he'd dealt with his cousin, Jake turned to Brenda and softened his voice. "Please go with him, and believe me, we're not an item. We're not dating and we're certainly not engaged. I'm not going to call you. We're not going to see each other."

Brenda put both hands on his chest and gave him a push. It was as effective as a kitten taking on a lion, but it seemed to make her feel better. She pranced to the car and jumped in.

Dwayne's first attempt to put the car in gear resulted in a stall. On the second try, the car leaped forward.

"If you strip those gears, I'll—" Jake's threat was lost in a cloud of dust as Dwayne and Brenda made their escape.

"The excitement's over. Now everyone can get back to whatever you were doing," Jake said, before he stomped off to the river.

THIS WAS a side of Jake CiCi had never seen before. He was always so laid-back and charming, except perhaps when he was dealing with Rondelle and crew, but even then he kept his cool. In fact, the only time she'd ever seen him lose his temper was during the infamous chicken incident, and that time he'd been provoked by the very same cousin. When Daddy blew his top, Jake had let it roll off his back. But his family obviously knew exactly how to push every one of his buttons.

Once the commotion died down and the kids were settled in for the night, CiCi adjourned to the kitchen for an orgy of chocolate cake. To her way of thinking, chocolate was the only civilized answer to an uncivilized problem.

She might as well admit it. She was incredibly attracted to Jake Culpepper, but no matter how she looked at it, it wasn't going to work. This episode with the blonde had put a final nail in that fantasy's coffin. And it brought her back to the question of whether famous men were actually capable of keeping their drawers up.

"Are you willing to share the goodies?"

She hadn't heard Jake come in, but there he was in the doorway, looking more luscious than a slab of gooey Texas sheet cake, and it didn't come much better than that.

"There's plenty. There's also milk in the fridge. After the day we've had, we deserve a treat." CiCi was determined to be cordial.

When Jake grinned, her heart went slam, bam, thank-you ma'am. Maybe there *was* something better than chocolate. If he could bottle that charm, he'd be able to put Snickers out of business.

Jake pulled the cake out of the refrigerator and cut himself a huge piece. "You've talked me into it."

"It's mandatory to have milk with chocolate." CiCi got up to find him a glass. "As a matter of fact, I'm fairly sure it's one of the commandments." She knew she was prattling, but did she care? Nope.

CALL HIM A PERV, but watching CiCi toy with the chocolate icing was giving Jake a hard-on that would make any red-blooded American man proud. However, lusting over the boss's daughter was out of the question. No telling what Texas Bob would do if Jake laid a pinkie on his "baby girl"— probably something nasty to a favorite part of his anatomy. And if that wasn't enough to silence Jake's pesky libido, he didn't know what was.

"It's been quite an afternoon, hasn't it?"

"Brenda told me why the tabloid guy was here," Jake said, forking up a bite of cake.

CiCi looked surprised. "Why?"

"Apparently, I'm a YouTube star."

"You are? What for?"

"Someone filmed Angel's rescue, and now Brenda says there's been something like three or four million hits."

"Million!" CiCi squeaked.

"Interesting, huh?"

"I wonder if Daddy has heard about this. I talked to him after Angel's rescue to let him know everything was okay. He wanted to come see for himself but I managed to forestall him. But with the YouTube thing, I suspect he'll make an appearance."

Jake was about to comment when the camp phone rang.

Another midnight call. He grabbed the phone before CiCi could come around the table and get it.

"Camp Touchdown."

WAS MERCURY in retrograde or what? All CiCi wanted was a piece of cake and a good night's sleep. Although stripping off Jake's Road Runner T-shirt and having her way with him was appealing, that was a nonstarter.

"Where?" Jake demanded. It was only one word, but it held a world of meaning. She'd been at camp just three weeks and already she'd had more excitement than she'd had in the past several years.

"When?" He gave her a look she couldn't quite read. "We'll be there in fifteen minutes."

It was Code Red time again.

"What is it?" CiCi was trying to keep her cool but knew she was failing miserably.

Jake propped his elbows on the table and put his head in his hands. "That idiot Rondelle and his friends snuck out and hitched a ride into town. I'm gonna kill that kid."

"Oh, great." CiCi felt herself deflate. Teenagers should come with a *Hazardous Cargo* sticker on their foreheads.

"It gets worse."

"How?" A lump formed in her throat and that meant tears weren't far behind.

"They got in a fight with some townies and the cops took all the underage combatants to juvenile detention."

Jake made a quick call to Greg, explaining the situation. He told the head counselor to commandeer the gardener's truck, again. It was a replay of the last Rondelle debacle, except this time the law was involved.

"No! No! No!" CiCi thumped her head on the table. She was tempted to beat herself senseless.

"It'll be fine, honest it will." Jake massaged the nape of her neck.

His touch was her undoing. It started with a sob, and then turned into a torrent of tears. CiCi wasn't crying because of some teenage antics. Instead, she suspected she was having a long-delayed reaction to the way her life was spiraling out of control. But whatever the reason, the tears kept flowing.

"Oh, God! Please don't cry. Please."

Jake sounded distraught and who could blame him? He hadn't signed on to deal with a full-blown lunatic.

"Come here."

A second later she found herself on his lap with her head cradled against his chest. He was rubbing gentle circles on her back as if comforting a small child.

The tears soon dried up, but she was hesitant to leave his arms. They felt so safe, and comfortable and right around her.

"Are you okay?" He tipped her chin up, hesitated for a moment and then slanted his lips over hers. The kiss started off as a soft exploration of her lips but quickly became an erotic exploration of her mouth, her heart and her soul.

Multicolored stars danced in front of CiCi's eyes as she tried, unsuccessfully, to catch her breath. Now she knew exactly what being ravaged meant—and hot damn, it was scrumptious.

"You are so beautiful," he muttered as he slowly inched her tank top up to reveal her breasts. Jake gently played with her nipples but quickly replaced his hands with that magical mouth of his, rubbing her midriff as he suckled.

Holy Mother!

CiCi was about to make a complete fool of herself when Jake pulled slowly away, putting his forehead against hers. "Believe me, I really hate to mention this, but we have to go."

"Why?" Then it hit her. Rondelle and his partners in crime were in trouble again. "Oh, right. Um, why don't you go on out? I'll be there in a second."

When she hazarded a glance in the mirror she almost croaked. There were some major repairs to be made before she'd be presentable.

"Good grief!" She had a red nose, smeared mascara, puffy

lips and hair that would give the Bride of Frankenstein a run for her money. CiCi touched her lips. How could Jake even want to kiss her, much less become intimately familiar with every inch of her body?

Chapter Twenty-One

CiCi couldn't believe she was sitting in Sheriff Johnson's office, waiting to post bail for a bunch of juvenile delinquents. Thank goodness Jake and Greg were with her.

"You seem so calm. I'm a nervous wreck." She couldn't stop wringing her hands. The anxiety had to be hormonal. That was it, her estrogen was overstimulated.

Jake's hands were folded across his stomach. "Looks can be deceiving."

"How long do you think it will take to process the little idiots?"

"I hope it's long enough to give them a scare. I suspect the good sheriff's sick of seeing us. So—" He leaned forward as if he had something important to say but when the lawman returned he sat back.

"Ms. Hurst, Mr. Culpepper. I'm sorry to keep you waiting. I talked to our District Attorney. We decided to give the kids a warning." He dropped a manila folder on his desk. "Lots of paperwork, you know. And I'm missing my soft bed. So you're free to take them home. A word of caution, though. I don't want to see them again. Ya' hear?"

CiCi was willing to guarantee he wouldn't. If Rondelle so much as sneezed in the next week and a half, he'd be on his way back to Houston. She was at her wits' end with that boy.

"You won't have any more trouble from us, I promise." She sent a couple of prayers heavenward. One, that she wasn't the biggest fool in central Texas. And two, that the little twit and his buddies would keep their noses clean and not make a liar out of her.

"Well, that's about it. You can retrieve the boys from the desk sergeant."

CiCi stood and extended her hand. "Thank you. I'll keep an eye on them, I promise."

Jake didn't say a word. He didn't have to. His frown said it all.

JAKE DIDN'T WANT to worry about sealed juvenile records, or hanging around a cop shop, waiting to bail anyone out. He'd extricated himself from that hole once and he didn't intend to go for a repeat. His family was enough to deal with. Other people's kids were *not* his problem.

And furthermore, Texas Bob could take his contract and cram it up his flabby white butt. If he didn't realize how valuable Jake was to the team that was his loss.

The ride back to camp took forever. CiCi was trying to keep up the conversation but Jake wasn't interested in talking. He was fed up with all the garbage.

All he wanted to do was pack his things and get back to his real life. And the first item on his new agenda was to cut Dwayne and Darrell loose. It was time for those boys to sink or swim.

Dwayne and Darrell had moved in with Jake and his mother in elementary school because their own mother was an on-again, off-again drug addict. She wasn't capable of raising two rambunctious little kids so Jake's mom had taken over the task, parenting the boys as though they were her own. Good old Darrell and Dwayne proved the adage that no good deed went unpunished.

Jake was out of the truck almost before it came to a stop. Reaming out Rondelle and crew would be his last act at Camp Touchdown.

"Get out. I have something to say." He didn't yell or curse or even act mad, but the teens got the message. All five boys jumped from the truck without a word. CiCi might be more inclined to hold hands and hum, but frankly he didn't care what she'd learned in that fancy university. He was pissed off and tired of the whole mess.

"I'm only going to say this once, so I hope you get it," Jake said, pacing up and down in front of the kids. "The path you're following is going to get you killed. If you're lucky, you'll just get thrown in jail." He put his hands on his hips. "We're not talking juvenile detention. We're talkin' hard time. You may think it's cool to be a wise guy, but believe me, it isn't."

Rondelle's expression was stony. The other boys looked like they were about to hurl.

"Ms. Hurst and her family have given you a golden opportunity with this camp and you—" he pointed at each of the boys "—have thrown it in her face. The fact is you're too stupid to be here. It's not my decision to make, but if it was, I'd send you home right now. That way, someone who deserves it could take your place. That's all I have to say."

He turned to CiCi. "They're all yours. I think I'll call it a night. If they give you any trouble, just give me a yell. I wouldn't mind having another little chat." He shot the teens a fiendish smile. "Do you guys understand?"

The band of scoundrels nodded in unison.

"Good. I don't appreciate anyone messin' with a friend of mine. And I consider Ms. Hurst a friend. Got it?"

They responded with another round of nods.

Jake hadn't even made it to his cabin before his cell chirped. When he checked the caller ID and saw that it was his agent, his stomach clenched. Larry Quinn wouldn't be calling him this late unless something bad had happened.

"What's wrong?" Jake skipped the preambles.

"You're not going to like this."

"What I don't like is when you start a conversation that way." Jake rubbed the bridge of his nose. This day was giving him a major headache.

"Dwayne couldn't get you, so he called me." Larry didn't bother to disguise his exasperation.

Jake's first reaction was panic. Had something happened to his mom?

"I have his number blocked. What's the problem?"

Larry paused. That was another bad omen. "Darrell's in the Bexar County jail in San Antonio. It's his third DUI."

"Crap!" Jake exclaimed. He'd bailed the idiot out twice in the past year.

"Dwayne wants you to post a bond for him."

Jake thought for a moment. It was time that his cousin discovered that breaking the law had consequences. "Do me a favor?"

"Name it and you've got it."

"Would you call a criminal defense attorney and make an appointment for me? In the morning will be fine. I think I'm going to let Darrell stew in jail for a while. It'll do him good."

Larry chuckled. "I suspect you're right. From what I hear, the county jail is a gnarly place." His agent wasn't fond of Jake's ne'er-do-well relatives. He'd spent almost as much time getting them out of trouble as Jake had.

"And would you make me a reservation at La Mansíon? Make it for a couple of days." The five-star hotel on the Riverwalk was awash in the ambiance of old San Antonio and would be just the escape Jake needed. "I'll leave bright and early tomorrow. I can meet with the lawyer after nine."

"You got it. I'll call you back with the time and place. Let me know if you need anything else."

"Right. Do you think a jury would convict me if I killed Darrell?"

"Don't do it. Your fifteen percent is one of the reasons I live so well."

"Screw you," Jake replied, his standard response to his agent's well-worn joke.

There was one last item on his agenda. He had to tell CiCi he needed a couple of days off, but certainly not why. She'd already met Dwayne; she didn't need to know about Darrell, too.

Chapter Twenty-Two

The next morning Jake pulled into the lot of the Broadway Diner on San Antonio's north side. He parked between a brand-new Mercedes and a beater pickup. With what lawyers charged per hour, the German number probably belonged to the cum laude Stanford graduate.

The aroma of comfort food greeted Jake like an old friend. Just thinking about breakfast made his stomach growl. Two customers were already seated at the old-fashioned counter—one in a suit, the other in a pair of faded jeans with a battered Stetson on the table. Not giving it a second thought, Jake headed toward the Marlboro man—this was Texas, after all.

"You must be Cedric Thompson." Jake hoped his intuition wasn't on the fritz.

"Nope, can't say that I am."

"I'm your guy." The man wearing the thousand-dollar suit and a gold Rolex stood and extended his hand. "Cedric Thompson, Esquire, at your service. Sit down and tell me what I can do for you."

"I'm sure Larry filled you in on the situation with my cousin."

"He certainly did, but I'd like to hear your thoughts," Cedric said. "As I understand it, he's in jail on his third DUI.

Bad boy. Your agent said you don't want to bail him out this time."

Before Jake could answer, the waitress appeared. He didn't bother consulting the menu before ordering. "Coffee, scrambled eggs, crisp bacon and grits, and double it all."

"Is that it?" she asked, scribbling down his order.

"Yes, ma'am."

She turned Jake's cup over and poured him a generous serving. "Here's your coffee. You order will be right up."

Jake waited until she moved on to the next customer before he continued. "It's not about the money. I want him to learn a lesson. His last few encounters with the law obviously haven't made an impression, and I'm afraid that's partially my fault. I've enabled him," Jake said with a sigh. "He's never had to suffer the consequences, and that has to stop now. Next time he might kill someone." He took a sip of coffee. "I can't have that on my conscience."

Cedric stared at him for a few seconds. "Good for you. If more family members thought the same way, we might have fewer repeat offenders. Most people are willing to refinance the house to get their relatives out of the clink."

"Are you sure you're a defense attorney? Most of you guys want to get your clients out of jail and to heck with guilt or innocence."

"That's what we're paid for. I have somewhat of a different viewpoint. If you're guilty there's a price to pay. I guarantee my clients a good defense but not a miracle." The lawyer pulled out his wallet. "But just so you know you're not getting a pig in a poke, here's my 'you're a smart boy and passed the bar' card. Just want you to be assured that I'm a bar-certified attorney."

Jake threw up his hands. "Hey, guy. I believe you."

"Good. Do you want to go see your cousin or do you want me to?"

"I think you should do it." Jake didn't know if he could visit Darrell without beating the snot out of him.

"I hate to seem avaricious, but I want to make sure that you're paying my bill, not your cousin."

"I'm paying."

"Good. You're my first football-player client. I'm a big Road Runner fan. So, what's the next season going to be like?"

If Jake knew that, he'd hire out as a soothsayer. "I'm a bit prejudiced, but I think our offense is pretty hot." Jake didn't bother to say that Texas Bob might not even pick up his option. If that happened, God only knew where he'd be playing.

Cedric leaned back. "I read about the team in the sports page." And then in a lightning-fast conversation change, he resumed his lawyer persona.

"How long are you willing to let Darrell stay in jail? Once his case goes to the judge, it's out of our hands. Right now we have two choices. We can bail him out or we can make sure he stays where he is, at least for the time being."

"I don't want him in there too long."

"In a couple of days there'll be an arraignment. That's when he can get out on his own recognizance. At least, that's what I'll argue for. If that doesn't work, do you think he can come up with a couple of hundred, or maybe even a thousand for the bail bondsman?"

If all else failed, Dwayne could get a job. If either of the cousins asked Mom for money, Jake would kill 'em. "I think so."

"Good. That's our game plan. When he comes up for trial, I'll try to get him probation. But in this state, a third DUI can land a guy in jail for six months."

"I guess that's a chance Darrell will have to take," Jake said, attacking his breakfast the waitress had just delivered. "Not to be trite, but if you do the crime, you'd better be willing to do the time."

Cedric smirked at Jake's use of the cliché. "That's what keeps me in business." He stood. "I'll call you after the arraignment."

"Sounds good to me. I'll talk to you soon."

Jake wasn't ready to return to Camp Touchdown, so he decided to spend the night in San Antonio, relaxing and soaking up the ambience. Now that he'd decided to cut his cousins loose, he had to come up with an implementation strategy, because Darrell and Dwayne were nothing if not persistent.

And then there was the problem of his attraction to CiCi Hurst. He could tell his head that she was out of his league, but his heart and other areas had a different idea. But when had he ever followed a safe course?

It was a beautiful evening, so he was out on the balcony with a frosty margarita in one hand and a nacho in the other, watching the gondolas float down the river and the tourists enjoy their stroll down the narrow sidewalks. If he could get CiCi to join him for a romantic weekend, that would be his idea of heaven.

A soft bed, spicy food, a little bubbly and a silky female— just thinking about it turned him on. Until he envisioned Texas Bob's ugly mug and he deflated like a three-day-old helium balloon. Plus, he could only imagine what CiCi would think if she saw where he grew up. And he wouldn't find out unless he went back to Camp Touchdown. So his escape plans had to take a backseat to a more important goal.

Jake was almost back to the camp the next morning when his cell rang. He checked the caller ID and thought about ignoring it, but a smart guy never blew off his mother.

"Hey, Mom, what's up?" He knew exactly what she wanted but it couldn't hurt to play dumb.

Bonnie Sue Culpepper was an expert at going straight for the jugular.

"Why aren't you bailing out your cousin?"

Dwayne must have spread the bull on nice and thick.

"If Darrell doesn't get his act together, he'll kill someone and I refuse to be responsible for that."

"Oh, dear. Did he have another DUI? Dwayne didn't tell me that."

Jake could almost see her hand pressed against her chest.

"Dwayne told me that he got in a little bar tiff and you refused to help."

Thank you, cousin. "Let's be blunt—Dwayne and Darrell are pathological liars. And this is the *third* time this year that Darrell's been picked up for drunk driving."

"Oh, no," she said with a sigh.

"Oh, yes. I got a lawyer, but Darrell's going to have to sit in jail for a couple of days. Then he and Dwayne can figure out how to make the bail money."

"I'm sure you know best," his mother said, although she didn't sound convinced.

"Mom, please don't give them any money."

"Are you sure that's the right thing to do?"

"No, but nothing else has worked. Darrell and Dwayne have to grow up."

"Are you coming home anytime soon?" Bonnie Sue asked, changing the subject.

"I'll be at Camp Touchdown for another week and a half. Then I have summer training camp. I promise I'll come by to see you soon." He wasn't sure when that would be, but he never broke a promise to his mom.

Chapter Twenty-Three

CiCi had been pondering the problem of Rondelle and his friends all night. True, they'd had their third strike and by all rights she should send them packing, but they'd seemed so contrite. She desperately wanted to talk to Jake, but he was in San Antonio. That left Daddy—not her first choice, but it was something she had to do.

It was eight o'clock before she made that dreaded call to Houston. The sheriff was involved in this one, and Daddy would be furious if she didn't keep him in the loop. Marianne answered on the first ring.

"Hi, Mama. Did I call too early?"

"Are you kidding? Your daddy was up before the sun. Swear to goodness, that man makes me crazy," she said with a laugh. "Is everything okay?" Her mom's intuition was clearly working well.

"We've had a problem with some of the campers. I'd like to talk to Daddy about it."

"Sure, I'll get him."

Daddy answered within thirty seconds. "What's wrong, baby girl?"

CiCi gave him a synopsis of the teens' antics. The camp was legally responsible for the kids—and sleazy lawyers and frivolous lawsuits were a dime a dozen—so

CiCi knew that Daddy would call his attorney as soon as they disconnected.

"I'll be there before noon. Don't worry, we'll take care of this." Texas Bob hung up before she could say word. But what would she say? I'm sorry, I screwed up? I'm so inept I can't even handle a bunch of kids?

Back to the immediate problem—what would she do with the little darlings until the cavalry came to the rescue? Then it came to her. She'd bore them to death.

CiCi found Greg having breakfast with his staff. She poured a cup of coffee and sat down. "I suppose you've all heard about what happened."

From the sheepish looks, CiCi knew that Rondelle and crew had been the topic of breakfast conversation.

"Yes, ma'am, we certainly did." A petite counselor was the first to speak up.

"I have an idea." CiCi didn't know if this would work, but it was all she had.

"What is it?" Greg asked.

"I think they need some intensive academics. Something they'll find really tedious. I'm talking a couple of days of sheer, agonizing boredom." She flashed a perky smile she didn't feel. "Does anyone have a suggestion?"

"Math." That suggestion was offered by a lanky criminal justice major.

"Oh, yes," the petite blonde dance major concurred. "That stuff puts me to sleep."

"Do we have any math majors?" CiCi had to squelch a laugh when Greg raised his hand. He looked like a math geek.

"Looks like you're elected. We'll offer them a day of trying to figure out if train A leaves station C fifteen minutes before train B leaves station D, and then factor in X miles per hour to decide which one gets to point E first."

Greg looked a bit green, but like a good boy, he agreed. "Okay, I'm game. I hope this works."

"So do I," CiCi agreed. "So do I."

IT WAS ALMOST TIME FOR LUNCH when Texas Bob and Mackenzie roared up in a brand-new black Hummer.

Mac hopped out of the truck and grabbed her sister in a hug that almost took CiCi's breath away. For a tiny little thing, she could give a major-league hug.

"When Daddy said he was driving up, I decided to come along."

"He told you what's happening, right?"

Mac made a face. "Yeah. He's already made an appointment with the sheriff, and he spent almost an hour on the phone with Jameson." Jameson Swift was the Hurst family lawyer and the attorney for the foundation. "He thinks our liability is limited because we provide adequate supervision. You and I both know those kids are sneaky little devils."

Mac had pegged that one right.

"Where did Daddy go?"

Mac pointed in the direction of the main lodge where Greg was conducting his algebra seminar in the dining hall—complete with whiteboard and dry-erase markers. "He said he's going to have a chat with the kids."

CiCi sprinted off, hoping to catch Texas Bob before he blew his stack. Much to her surprise, she found him talking quietly to the teens. And even more startling, they seemed to be listening.

She sat down to hear what he had to say. Texas Bob could spin a tall tale with the best of them. According to him he'd had to walk two miles uphill each way to school—in the snow. Oh, puleeze, the man grew up in South Texas. His next white lie was that he started with nothing but a dream and ten bucks in his pocket. Grandma Hurst would bust a gut on that one.

He went on to say that if he could make something of himself, the boys could, too.

Texas Bob ended his talk with, "I know this was your third strike, and letting you off probably isn't a smart idea. But you caught me on a good day. However—" he glared at each kid separately "—this is a one-time deal. Sorta like the red-light special sales at my car lot. You screw this up and you're gone. You won't ever be able to come back. Got it?"

The kids nodded. They were getting good at that nodding thing.

"Glad to hear it. I'm countin' on ya. I know you won't let me down. Right?"

Rondelle was the first to speak. "Yes, sir. We understand." He looked at his compatriots. They all gave an affirmative thumbs-up. Texas Bob might look like a big teddy bear, and he might act like a buffoon sometimes, but he wasn't anyone's fool.

"Now I'm taking my girls to lunch. CiCi, where's your sister?"

"She's outside." Lunch? Was that a euphemism for having a chat with the sheriff?

The minute they walked out the door, Texas Bob reverted to Winston Hurst—all business. "Where's Culpepper?"

"He said there was a family emergency so he went to San Antonio last night."

"He'd better not be pulling a fast one."

"I don't think so. He was really upset when he left."

Daddy shrugged. "In that case I guess it's okay. We're meeting Sheriff Johnson at the Starlight Diner." He gave his daughter a wink. "They have the best chicken-fried steak I've ever put in my mouth. And you know I parley a whole lot better when I'm full. It never hurts to have a good relationship with the law." Actually, he negotiated quite well under any circumstance.

On impulse, CiCi kissed her dad's cheek. "I love you, Daddy. I'm sorry things got so messed up. I didn't want to disappoint you."

Texas Bob put his hands on her shoulders. She was tall, but he still had six inches on her. "Sweetheart, you've never disappointed me. I'm so proud of my girls I almost pop my buttons every time I see one of you." He emphasized that by squeezing her tight.

So that's where Mac had learned to do the bear hug.

WHILE TEXAS BOB AND THE SHERIFF were talking, CiCi and Mac indulged in a girl chat.

"Do you know why Jake went to San Antonio?" Mac asked.

"Not really. He said he had a family emergency and I believe him." There was that niggle of a doubt, but even if he had a harem of curvaceous women why should it matter to her?

Mac obviously realized this wasn't a safe topic, so she went on to another. "I can't wait until you get home. There's something I want to talk to you about."

CiCi was also in need of sisterly venting, but she wasn't sure that was a good idea. All her thoughts were about Jake Culpepper. The problem was she didn't exactly know what to say. Was she the victim of unrequited lust or was it something more profound?

The only interest Jake had shown in her was some flirting and a couple of kisses. Fine, so they'd made out in the kitchen but that didn't mean they had a relationship.

She had only a few days left to make Jake want her, or fall in love with her, or whatever. Wait a minute! She'd been there and done that—married a jock who got tons of female attention, and had her heart broken. Sheesh! She was losing her mind again.

"I'll be home soon. We can get caught up on all my gossip then." That should give her some breathing room. "So what do you want to talk to me about? I'm dying of curiosity."

Mac was a true blonde with the tendency to blush. And when she did, it was something to behold. Her normal alabaster skin didn't turn a nice rosy pink. On the contrary, she was the only person CiCi had ever known who could actually get fire-engine red.

"Good Lord. What's the problem?" She hoped it wasn't what she was thinking

"You remember when I told you about my Starbucks dates with Cole?" Mac answered, somehow managing to get redder by the minute.

CiCi was almost afraid to ask. "Did something else happen?"

"Not exactly." Mac's hesitancy told her everything she didn't want to know.

"So what *exactly* did you do?" She held her hands up like a Stop sign. "Wait. I don't want any specifics."

"It's probably what you think." Mac rubbed her forehead. "I do need some advice. But it can wait until you get home. I'm not planning to do anything silly in the meantime."

Thank God! Of all the people who shouldn't get involved with an athlete, Mac was at the top of the list.

But who was she to talk? Her name would be in the number two spot.

Chapter Twenty-Four

It was almost noon the next day before CiCi saw Jake pull into the camp driveway and head straight for his cabin. He was normally upbeat, but when he left for a run just a few minutes after his arrival he seemed ready to chew nails. Whatever was happening wasn't good.

Almost two hours later, CiCi wandered down to the river and saw Jake sitting under the big oak. Against her better judgment, she strolled out to join him. This was either going to be the biggest mistake of her life or the best thing she'd ever done.

Jake was at the picnic table with his head in his hands, the picture of dejection. His hair was still wet from a shower.

"Do you want some company?" she asked, still not sure she was doing the right thing.

"Yeah, sure." He scooted over to make room for her on the bench.

This was a pregnant pause if ever CiCi had known one. "Is there anything I can do for you?"

Jake glanced at her almost as if he'd forgotten she was sitting there. "I'm sorry. I didn't mean to be rude when I left without any explanation. I had some family stuff to take care of."

It didn't appear he was going to elaborate so it was up to

CiCi to keep the conversation going. "Daddy and Mac drove up yesterday."

"They did?" That got his attention.

"He said he wanted to talk to the sheriff about Rondelle and the others, but I suspect he wanted to see how I was doing. He's a bit overprotective."

Jake laughed. "You don't say!"

He laughed—that was encouraging.

"I think he'd like to have us cloistered. Heaven help Molly when she hits her teens."

Jake shot her an assessing look. "You're lucky to have such a nice family." He chuckled mirthlessly. "Although I'm not sure *nice* describes Texas Bob, but I suppose he tries."

"He really is a kind man, although he can be a bit over the top."

CiCi didn't know what to say next, so she welcomed the silence.

Jake was the first to speak. "My mom was a single parent. She worked two jobs to keep us afloat. Regardless of how much we were struggling she gladly took in my two cousins when their mother dumped them. She couldn't bear to see them lost in the foster system, especially when there were relatives who could do the job. She never had it easy, but now that I have money, she has a nice home and no financial worries."

"That's kind of you." CiCi didn't know where this was going, so she kept her response brief.

"I went to San Antonio because my cousin Darrell was in jail and I needed to talk to an attorney."

"I'm sorry. What happened?"

"He's stupid, that's what happened."

For a moment CiCi thought he'd leave it at that. Then he continued with his story.

"Darrell has a drinking-and-driving problem and he got

busted for the third time. I decided that instead of bailing him out, I'd leave him in jail for a while. Once he goes to court, it's out of my hands." Jake turned to look at her. "Personally, I think he needs to get scared silly."

CiCi reached for his hand. She could tell that his decision, right or wrong, was weighing on him.

"Darrell and Dwayne have been hell-raisers since they hit puberty. I've bailed them out of so many scrapes I can't even count them all. I am so tired of it," he said with a deep sigh.

"And that's why the situation with Rondelle and his friends has bothered you so much."

"Yeah. Sometimes I feel like I'm swimming upstream. Guess it's too bad you can't choose your family."

CiCi really couldn't relate. If she had the choice, she'd pick her family every time. Without thinking about it, she wrapped her arm around Jake's waist. This man needed a hug and that was one thing the Hurst family did really well.

IT HAD BEEN A TERRIBLE WEEKEND. Even at his best, Darrell wasn't exactly pleasant, and when he didn't get his way he was downright horrible. Jake could only imagine how his cousin had reacted to the news that Jake wasn't going to bail him out again.

However, things were definitely looking up. Jake wondered if CiCi realized she'd moved from rubbing his back to caressing his neck. He didn't know if it meant anything, or if it was simply her way of comforting him. Whatever it was, he liked it. In fact—try as he might to avoid it—he liked her, a lot.

When her hand slipped down to the small of his back, Jake felt his temperature elevate. He'd been seduced by women who were far more experienced, but CiCi's touch was real and honest.

Deep down, Jake knew that what he was about to do was a mistake, but his good sense and his need for love were duking it out. Fortunately—or perhaps unfortunately—his heart won.

"I'm probably going to regret this," he muttered, pulling CiCi close. She smelled like spring, rainwater, and all things girly. It was an incredible aphrodisiac. He nuzzled her neck, breathing in the scent of her hair. It was as if his body had decided on a course of action all on its own. If he had half a brain, he wouldn't be nibbling on her earlobe. She was still the boss's daughter. But for now, he just didn't care.

Jake shifted on the bench and settled her in his lap. That was better—much, much better. It gave him perfect access to everything he wanted to touch, see, caress and kiss. He started with her neck. He'd always been a sucker for a beautiful neck and CiCi's was gorgeous.

Goose bumps danced on her beautiful skin in the wake of the slow, warm kisses he placed down her shoulder. The thought of having her naked in his bed was wreaking havoc with his mind, not to mention his sex drive.

A noise nearby brought the real world back into focus. What was he thinking? They were in a public place. Kids could walk by.

Apparently CiCi realized the same thing. "Oh, my God!"

Jake was having an "oh, my God" experience, too, but he didn't think she meant it in quite the same way he did.

She jumped off his lap. Damn, she was cute.

Chapter Twenty-Five

CiCi's face was on fire. She didn't blush very often, but if there was ever an appropriate time, this was it. What was wrong with her? They were in the middle of the camp and she was letting Jake have his way with her. They'd crossed the line from friendly hug to full-on making out when camp rules strictly prohibited staff from all public displays of affection—and she hadn't been turned on like that in ages... maybe ever.

She wondered if he felt the same way, or if this was strictly a one-way street. If they hadn't been interrupted, heaven only knows what would have happened. With that thought in mind, CiCi fanned herself.

"I have a ton to do, so I'd better get hopping." Great, now she sounded like a British spinster. "I'm sorry about your cousin, and if it's any comfort I think you did the right thing."

"I do, too." Jake smiled and then sauntered off.

Crumb! CiCi was horny as all hell. Celibacy—what had she been thinking? Long before she and Tank split, their love life hadn't exactly been earth-shattering. Scrub that—it had been the pits. Probably because he'd been too busy practicing Kama Sutra positions with his librarian friend.

God, she'd love a glass of wine, but coffee, and lots of it, would have to do. If it hadn't been fifty miles to the nearest Starbucks, she'd be in her car and on her way.

She'd acted like a virgin bride when Jake had done nothing more than kiss her— Oh, right, there was that little bit of petting. So why not ask him to go to lunch and get this relationship, or whatever it was, back on a professional basis. Plus there was an espresso stand in town and what she wouldn't give for a cappuccino.

Jake was coaching softball when she finally found him. He bent over to pick up a ball, allowing her an amazing view of his buns of steel. Whew! That was certainly enough to get her all hot and bothered.

Lunch. All she wanted to do was have lunch with the guy— not ravish him.

"Hey, Jake," she called, motioning him over. "Do you have time to go for lunch?"

"Sure. Once I'm done this session, I've got a free afternoon. When do you want to go?"

"How about an hour?"

"I'm all yours."

CiCi only wished—or did she?

THE RIDE INTO Kerrville was fairly quiet. CiCi wasn't quite sure what she wanted to say, and ended up making trivial small talk.

"Have you ever been to the Cedar?" she asked.

"Can't say that I have. What is it?"

"It's a dive but it's been around for at least a century so it's a historical landmark. Bank robbers from the thirties used it as their watering hole."

"Am I going to have to fight my way out of the place?"

"I don't think so," CiCi said, and then muttered, "I hope not."

CiCi wasn't exaggerating about the Cedar. It was so old Davy Crockett had probably been a regular. And the line of Harleys out front was only one clue that this wasn't a ladies' lunch venue. Jake had been to more than his share of places like this but he was surprised CiCi even knew they existed.

The inside was even worse than the exterior. It was dark and smelled like decades of stale beer. The dented picnic tables and mismatched benches looked like a throwback to the cattle drives of the nineteenth century. Except now the cowboys had been replaced with Born to Raise Hell bikers.

The minute they walked in, at least a dozen pair of eyes latched on to CiCi's backside. Jake might have to fight their way out of here, after all. He led the way to a table at the rear of the tavern. Their best bet was to be as inconspicuous as possible.

Thanks to his trailer-park background, Jake's taste ran more to bar food than to five-star restaurants, but even for him this was iffy. He wiped ketchup off the plastic menu.

"What do you recommend?" he asked, wondering if CiCi had been here before.

"Burgers, definitely the burgers. See the 'Blow the Top off Your Head' burger?" She pointed to an item toward the bottom of the page. "Daddy loves that one. They load on the jalapeños. It's a bit hot for me but you might like it."

"Texas Bob comes here?"

"It's one of his favorite places. They have homemade French fries, and the onion rings are to die for."

The potbellied bartender strolled over. "What can I do for you folks?" he asked, then squinted at CiCi. "Miz Hurst, it's sure good to see you. How's your daddy?"

"He's fine. I'll tell him you asked. How's the chili today?"

"I'd stick with the burgers if I was you."

"Okay, I'll take my regular with an order of fries and onion rings on the side."

The man turned to Jake and did the squinty thing again. "Aren't you Jake Culpepper?"

"Yep."

"Hot damn! Hey, boys, this here is Jake Culpepper."

So much for anonymity.

AFTER JAKE SIGNED a variety of T-shirts, ball caps and coasters the crowd finally dispersed.

"Don't you get tired of that?" CiCi asked.

"Sometimes. If we have a losing season I'm almost afraid to go to the post office. But I'm sure you know all about that from being married to Tank." Jake shrugged. "Sometimes it's a pain, but we're in the entertainment business, so it's part and parcel of the game."

CiCi hadn't quite thought of it that way. "What about the women?"

"What women?"

"The ones who want you to autograph their…their ta-tas."

Jake laughed so hard she was afraid he was going to fall off his chair. "I can honestly say I've never been asked to sign anyone's ta-tas." When CiCi didn't join in, he got serious. "That really bothers you, doesn't it?"

She sighed. "It does. Tank always had women coming on to him. At first I thought it was funny, but after he started taking them up on it, it stopped being humorous."

Jake rubbed his chin. "I have to confess something."

That sounded ominous.

"When I first met you I assumed you were a stuck-up debutante, but given what I know of you now—including this place—I was wrong. So I guess we both have our share of hang-ups."

"Why would you think I was a snob?"

"Because you have money."

"So do you." She was about to get irritated.

"And you made fun of my truck."

"What?"

"That day I came by your house, you thought I was the gardener."

"I don't even remember that!"

Jake took her hand. "Let me tell you a sad story." His grin didn't match his words.

"I've been dirt poor all my life, and when I went to A&M on a football scholarship I thought I had it made. I still didn't have any money, but I was on my way up. And then I met this girl—a Dallas deb." Jake sighed. "To make a long story short the minute she met Dwayne she dropped me. I'd already put a diamond on layaway, just waiting for the perfect moment." He took a big swallow of beer. "That's my sad story."

"So I guess I have to come up with something, too?"

"Not if you don't want to."

CiCi grimaced. "I will confess that I wanted to pull Brenda's bleached blond hair out by the roots."

Jake responded with a belly laugh. "I'd pay good money to see that."

"I'm serious. She was so, beautiful, and I'm not."

Jake looked up with a start. "What did you say?"

"About what?"

"About your looks?"

"I'm not blond and busty and…" CiCi shrugged. "And I don't have big hair."

Jake whooped. "You're hilarious. You could shave your head and I wouldn't care. I'd still think you're beautiful." He waggled an eyebrow. "In fact, you'd look damned sexy that way."

Jake scooted over next to her on the bench. "I didn't invite

Dwayne and Brenda to the camp. I dated her for about a month a little while ago and she became obsessed. It was kind of freaky, and she didn't take the breakup well. Nevertheless, I'm sorry."

Jake ran his fingers through her hair. The next she knew she was in his arms and he was making a thorough exploration of her mouth. That was more like it.

"I love you just the way you are," he murmured between kisses.

Holy tamale! Had he honest-to-goodness used the L word? Did he mean it or was it just a figure of speech? And should she ask him?

That question was forestalled by the arrival of their food. Nothing like rescue by French fry.

Chapter Twenty-Six

CiCi had assumed she'd see Jake at breakfast but he was a no-show—nor was there any sign of him for the rest of the morning.

"Do you think he's avoiding me?" she asked Sugar Plum. The dog answered by plastering herself against CiCi's leg.

"Oh, well, when in doubt do paperwork." But first things first—she needed a fresh cup of coffee. With a mug in one hand and a doughnut in the other, CiCi marched to her office, intent on getting some work done, or at least on putting Jake Culpepper out of her mind.

Two hours later she was ready for a break so she grabbed a Coke and went out to the porch. She had closed her eyes and was meditating when Jake came up and rocked her world with a kiss.

"You look so comfortable I thought I'd join you." He sat down in the adjacent twig rocker. "What are you thinking about?"

"That you might be avoiding me."

"No way. I've been up to my eyebrows in kid problems this morning. This camping experience was supposed to be about schmaltzy songs and swimming parties, not bailing kids out of the clink."

"What do you think we should—" CiCi didn't have a chance to finish before Angel ran up, obviously upset.

"Ms. Hurst, I've…I've got a problem." The fifteen-year-old managed to get that much out before she burst into tears.

"Oh, honey." CiCi pulled her into a hug, looking over the teen's head, seeking Jake's guidance. There was never a dull moment at Camp Touchdown.

"What happened?" he asked.

It took a while before Angel's tears subsided into a few sniffles and a deep sigh.

"I'm sorry, Coach." She tried to giggle but the attempt fell short. "I know guys hate it when girls cry."

Jake ruffled her hair. "Why don't you tell us what's going on, and start at the beginning."

Angel took a deep breath. "The last time I talked to my mom was after that river…thingy. Normally she's pretty good about calling my cell, but I haven't heard from her in a couple of days." The teen sniffled. "I just got a call from our neighbor. She said that my mom and her boyfriend have been busted on meth charges. I don't know what to do."

CiCi didn't have a clue what to think or say.

"Is that all she said?" Jake asked.

Angel nodded. "Uh-huh."

"Does your dad live in Houston?"

"I…uh…don't know who he is."

CiCi's heart broke for her. This wonderful young lady had a druggie mother and an unidentified father. She had to wonder whether kids like Angel had any chance at a productive life.

"CiCi, why don't you take Angel to find a cold drink? I have some calls to make." Jake winked at them both. "Angel, I know some folks who may be able to help."

DAMN IT TO HELL! Jake thought as he punched in the number of a friend who specialized in family law. Why did irresponsible people have kids? He'd seen this situation way too often—a nice child saddled with crappy parents, or in this case, a single mom.

Angel's mother had a live-in, meth-cooking boyfriend. People who cleaned up meth labs worked in Hazmat suits, but druggies didn't seem to care what kind of nasty environment they subjected their kids to.

The question was whether Angel would be better off with her mother or in the foster care system. If Jake could answer that, he'd be on his way to sainthood.

"Hey, I have a big favor to ask," he said when his friend Josh answered.

"Are you going to pay me, or is this a freebie?" Josh responded.

"Since when have you ever done anything for free?"

"Not often. So, what's up?"

Jake filled him in on the details. "I need you to go to the jail and talk to the mother. If you think she's retrievable, see what you can do to get her bailed out. Let her know that your representation is contingent on ditching the boyfriend. If she agrees, and you think she's serious, I'd like you to represent her."

"I'll do what I can. Keep in mind that I'm going to charge you my overtime rates," Josh said with a laugh.

"Whatever. I don't want this kid to be foisted off on the state. Camp is over in a week and she needs someplace to live."

"Right on. I'll call you when I have some answers."

Jake disconnected. He hoped his friend was a miracle worker because that's what this one was going to need.

Chapter Twenty-Seven

It was Saturday before Angel's mom was bailed out. They were in the last week of camp but that didn't mean that everything had calmed down. All Jake wanted was some downtime from the brouhaha, and that came when he managed to sneak away for a picnic with CiCi.

"Did you know that you can get into some itchy stuff sitting on the ground?" he asked as he spread out their blanket.

"Yep, I learned that one the hard way," CiCi said with a laugh. "That's why I've slathered on enough insect repellent to discourage an army of insects. They don't stand a chance."

"We'll see." Jake didn't bother to stifle his grin.

Lunch consisted of chicken-salad sandwiches, peach cobbler and iced tea. It was perfect cuisine for a lazy summer day.

Life was good—especially since he had a beautiful woman by his side—but there was a lingering sense of unfinished business. Where was this relationship going? Was it possible to get past the obvious differences in their background? There was only one way to tell, and that was for Jake to introduce CiCi to his childhood.

"Can you take a day off for a road trip?" He kissed the back of her neck.

"Of course, everyone deserves a day off. But it depends on

what you're thinking. If it has anything to do with food, I'm your girl."

Jake shrugged in the way that meant he wasn't completely comfortable with the situation. "We can eat, sure."

"I love your enthusiasm." CiCi tempered her sarcasm with a smile.

"I want to take you to San Antonio. There's, uh, there's something I want to show you. But afterward we can go to any restaurant that suits your fancy. How about it?"

"You make it hard to resist." She suspected this trip was about much more than finding the perfect taco.

"When?"

He gave her the sheepish grin she'd grown to love. "I thought we'd leave in the morning and come back Monday. Can Greg handle everything for a day?"

"I'm sure he can." That was the least of her worries. Right now, spending the night with Jake was at the top of her list.

THE TRIP into San Antonio took almost an hour and a half. On the way they bypassed the ritzy malls and ignored a veritable United Nations of restaurants without so much as slowing down.

CiCi managed to curb her curiosity until Jake took an exit into a part of town that had seen better days—or perhaps not. It wasn't exactly the barrio, but it was darned close.

It did, however, possess a certain charm featuring street vendors hawking tacos, storefronts displaying religious icons and a bustling mercado where menudo was probably more common than prime rib.

"Where are we going?" She turned in her seat to look at him, hoping his expression would give her a clue about what he was thinking.

"You'll see." Jake was clenching his jaw so tightly she was afraid he'd crack a molar. He also had a strangle-hold on the steering wheel. He hadn't exactly been chatty until now, but if he was going for the strong, mysterious type, she would, too.

CiCi's silent treatment lasted until Jake turned down a gravel lane. An industrial-size mailbox stood on one side of the road and a rusted sign reading Happy Trails was on the other.

"Happy Trails?"

He shot her an indecipherable look. "It's a trailer park."

"Okay." What was she supposed to say? Lots of people lived in manufactured homes.

"Here we are." Jake pulled up in front of a row of run-down single-wide trailers. This place had likely had its heyday in the fifties, but considering the cars on blocks, listing lean-to additions, gang-sign graffiti and lawns burned brown by the relentless sun that might be an overly generous assessment.

Happy Trails was light years away from CiCi's West Houston neighborhood, where lawns were manicured like putting greens and windows gleamed.

Jake pointed at a trailer that had likely once been a garish turquoise but was now badly faded. The front steps tilted precariously to one side and the entire structure looked ready to fall over.

"That's where I grew up." He said it so matter-of-factly that it took CiCi a few seconds to get a handle on what he said. And another moment to realize he was testing her.

He grew up here—so what? As far as she was concerned he could have been raised by wolves and it wouldn't matter.

"And?"

He seemed at a loss for words. "*That* was my home." He stabbed his finger toward the trailer. "There!"

"Yeah. I get it." If he wanted a pity party, he was on his own.

"I—" Jake was interrupted by furious knocking on the driver's side window.

Their visitor was a tiny gnome of a woman, so short she could barely reach the glass.

Without saying a word, Jake jumped out of the SUV and grabbed her in a bear hug. "How's the prettiest girl in south San?"

"You silly boy." The gnome whacked him on the arm. "I was wondering if you were gonna to sit out here all day. Get your butt on inside, ya hear." She peeked around Jake. "Brush off you manners, boy. Introduce me to your pretty young lady."

"Aunt Pallie, this is CiCi. CiCi, Aunt Pallie practically raised me." He gave the tiny woman a kiss on her wrinkled cheek.

"Come inside, gal. It's hot as blue blazes out here," Aunt Pallie demanded. It wasn't the most affable invitation CiCi had ever received, but she wouldn't miss this for the world.

"Yes, ma'am," she answered, with a grin at Jake.

"Young man, don't you do any lollygagging." Aunt Pallie cackled. She reached down to pick up a microscopic Chihuahua CiCi hadn't even noticed. "I'll go pour us some iced tea."

CiCi climbed out of the truck before Jake could come around to her door. His old-fashioned manners didn't seem to match his appearance and profession, but she thought they were charming.

Pallie's trailer was a stark contrast to the rest of the neighborhood. Not only was it fairly new, it was also meticulously maintained. Another incongruity was the bright red Mini Cooper parked under the adjacent carport.

CiCi thought she detected a pattern emerging—one that involved the big lug who was following her up the steps.

"You have a nice yard."

"I like to garden," the old woman said. "The yard's small, but it's a good size for me." The area inside the picket fence was barely larger than a postage stamp, but with its abundance of flowering plants, it almost felt like an English garden.

"Get yourselves on in here," she said, shepherding CiCi and Jake inside. "Have a seat on the couch."

Pallie started tidying up even though there wasn't a speck of dirt to be seen. "Lord have mercy, it's an oven out there. Hope you don't mind dogs. Chico's right partial to pretty young ladies." As if on cue, the dog cozied up next to CiCi.

"I'll fix us some sweet tea." Pallie shuffled off to the miniscule kitchen.

"Let me help you. I know where the Oreos are." Jake was grinning like a mischievous kid.

"About time you offered. You were actin' like company," Pallie said, tweaking his ear. With their disparity in height, that was something of an accomplishment.

CiCi wondered about their relationship. Jake treated Pallie like a grandmother, but considering she had skin the color of dark caramel, that wasn't likely.

Jake placed a tray of goodies on the coffee table. "Like I said, Pallie practically raised me. When I was fourteen, I decided it would be cool to be in a gang." He smiled fondly at his old friend. "She quickly disabused me of that notion."

"I whaled the dickens out of him, that's what I did. By the time he was eight he was bigger than me. But I was a whole bunch meaner." Pallie chuckled with humor. "This boy here kept those ne'er-do-well cousins out of trouble, too. Did you know that?"

"I didn't do quite as well as I wanted."

"You kept 'em mostly out of jail. And to my way of thinkin' that was an accomplishment. How are they?"

Jake laughed. "Dwayne is the reason I met CiCi." He told Pallie the story of the chicken.

By the time he finished, Aunt Pallie was laughing so hard tears were running down her wrinkled cheeks. "That rascal was always up to something. As bad as he was, I miss him."

An hour later, CiCi's blood sugar was through the roof, thanks to a combination of sweet tea and Oreos.

"I hate to say this, Aunt Pallie, but we'd better get going," Jake told their hostess.

"Chico's gonna surely miss you, Miss CiCi, but if you gotta go, you gotta go." Pallie followed them out to the SUV. "Give me a hug," she demanded, and Jake obliged. "You, too." CiCi gladly complied. "Don't be scarce now, ya hear?"

"Yes, ma'am." Jake gave Aunt Pallie a kiss and another hug.

It was almost six o'clock before they pulled onto the freeway. "I don't know about you, but I need some real food. How would you feel about some of the best Mexican food in the state?" Jake suggested.

"That sounds perfect." After the visit to Aunt Pallie's, CiCi could only imagine where they'd be dining. And when Jake pulled into the parking lot of a seedy-looking strip mall she knew she'd called that one right.

The café's décor was strictly thrift shop—mismatched tables and chairs, oilcloth table coverings and a menu written on a blackboard—but the aroma was enough to make CiCi's mouth water. And forget about English being the primary language. She felt as if she'd been transported to Guadalajara.

They were barely in the door when the owner spotted them. "Jake Culpepper, amigo, where have you been?" The man didn't even reach Jake's chin. "You too good to come eat with Juan?" He tempered his insult with a huge grin. Not waiting for an answer, and oblivious to the stares from other customers, he yelled. "Mama! Come out here. Jake's finally home."

"Mama" came out, wiping flour from her hands. "Juan

Martinez, stop that bellowing." She was a small woman and so pregnant that she seemed as round as she was short.

It appeared that Juan was about to get ripped a new one, but then "Mama" caught sight of Jake.

"You handsome devil, where have you been?" She got up on tiptoe and kissed his cheek, leaving a smudge of white behind. "Bad, bad boy, you haven't been home in ages." She smiled coyly. "If you ask me real nice, I'll ditch him and run off with you."

"Marcelita, you're as gorgeous as ever."

Jake patted his friend's belly. "How's Junior doing?"

"He's doing gymnastics. It wasn't like this with the girls," she said, placing her hand on her back.

"CiCi, I'd like to introduce you to my friends Juan and Marcelita Martinez. We grew up together."

CiCi wondered how he was going to describe her. Girlfriend? Wannabe lover? Boss?

"And this is my really good friend, CiCi Hurst."

What did *that* mean?

After the introductions, Juan took them to the party room in the back of the restaurant and produced a mountain of food. Periodically during the five-course meal, Juan and/or Marcelita would join them, exchanging stories and reminisces with Jake.

"How's your mom?" Juan asked as he and Marcelita brought in another round of mouth-watering food.

"She's okay. You know I bought her that house in the Woodlands near Houston. Now she's working at the cosmetics counter at Dillard's. It's something to keep her busy."

"You're a good son."

"I try."

"How about those no-good cousins?"

Jake shook his head. "Dwayne lives in Houston now and hasn't changed much. He stole my car a few weeks ago."

Juan exchanged a look with his wife.

"And Darrell is currently in the Bexar County jail. He just got his third DUI. Frankly, I hope he has to serve some time for this one."

"Amen. That would be a blessing." Juan made a sign of the cross.

"Juan and Darrell used to be best friends," Jake explained to CiCi. "They got into a lot of scrapes together. Aunt Pallie is responsible for keeping us all out of Huntsville." He was referring to the infamous state prison.

On that not-so-cheery note they finished their meal. Even though the cousins weren't physically present, they'd still managed to put a damper on the fun. With a chorus of "come back soon" and "we'll be watching the games," CiCi and Jake left the restaurant.

Fifteen minutes into the drive, her curiosity got the best of her. "Where are we going?"

Jake's expression remained shuttered, giving nothing away. "Uh, I thought we might spend the night here since we don't have to be back at camp until morning," he said, keeping his eyes on the road.

This was the point of no return. Was it time to take that next step?

"Are you thinking of two rooms or one?" CiCi knew exactly what he had in mind, but for some reason she couldn't help teasing him.

Jake took the exit toward downtown and pulled into a valet parking lot. He stopped the SUV and gave her one of those "oh, shucks" grins. "We can get two, if that's what you want. But I have to tell you that I hope that's not what you're going to say."

"Really?" CiCi couldn't resist the giggle that was bubbling up.

"Yeah." Jake looked a bit chagrined, but maintained his drop-dead smile.

"It would be my honor to share a room with you."

"Hot damn!"

Chapter Twenty-Eight

CiCi had never given much thought to seduction, but she was willing to give it a try. And somehow she managed to pull off the striptease. Piece by piece, she alluringly (she hoped) removed her clothing with a bare shoulder here, a provocative pose there.

She wasn't quite sure it was working, until she got a good look at Jake's face. He was in terrible pain. Poor, poor man, and wasn't that wonderful?

"I can't take any more of this. Come here." He pulled her into his arms and she continued to strip, except this time he was an active participant.

Jake was a man with a slow hand—a very slow hand that instinctively knew where to stroke and caress and gently tweak. Making love with him was alternatively hot and tantalizing and hard and fast. In other words, it was perfect.

THE SEX WAS AMAZING. Nope, that was too mild a description. It was so mind-blowing Jake thought he was going to stroke out. And now CiCi was curled up against him like a contented kitten. Her head was on his shoulder and her hand was doing wicked things with his chest hair.

"That was nice," she purred.

He propped himself up on one elbow. "Nice? I almost keeled over and you're calling it nice!"

"Actually, I've never experienced anything quite like it."

"Really?"

"No kidding."

"So…" He gave her a hopeful grin. "Are you ready to see if practice makes perfect."

"Oh, yeah. That sounds *nice*," she murmured, and that was the last intelligible sound she made for quite a while.

THEY WERE DRESSED in matching fluffy bathrobes and enjoying a fajita dinner from room service when CiCi took him by surprise. "Did I pass?"

Jake paused in the middle of slathering salsa on his tortilla. "Pass what?"

"Pass the test." She took a sip of her margarita and waited for his answer.

"I don't know what you're talking about." He figured when in doubt, go with a white lie.

"Oh, please. You took me to the trailer park to see if I passed the snob test. Don't try to deny it."

He was toast. "Well, uh…"

"I'll take that as a yes." She lifted her glass in salute. "I'm insulted but not enough to send you packing." She whacked him on the arm. "I like you, silly. Your background made you the man you are, and to that I say good going."

If Jake hadn't been in love with her before, he was now. Head over heels, knee-knocking in love. And that was scary as all hell. He couldn't come up with a response so he put down his fork, determined to show her exactly how he felt. They adjourned to the bed for some nonverbal communication.

Much later, Jake decided it was time to initiate a conversation that might be uncomfortable, but was necessary at this point in their relationship.

"Would you like to tell me about your marriage?"

MAC WAS THE ONLY ONE who knew the whole sordid story, but CiCi realized it was time to share. "I told you that he was sleeping with a librarian and left me. But that's not totally accurate. I think he mentally checked out long before he made his first visit to the Lincoln County Library." CiCi shrugged, thinking about the way their marriage had started unraveling shortly after their first anniversary.

"We had completely different goals and desires. I wanted a baby, he didn't. I wanted a job, he wanted me at home. I wanted to spend more time with my family, he didn't like them." She paused. "I gave in more than I should have. To be completely honest, I made more than my share of mistakes, too. But that's okay and I'm fine now. Actually, I'm doing amazingly well."

"I'm glad to hear it." Jake expressed his appreciation with a kiss.

"Not to be trite, but turnabout is fair play." CiCi snuggled up close. "Tell me more about your family."

For a moment she thought Jake hadn't heard her. He cleared his throat before answering. "My mom and dad never got married. I think he already had a wife, but Mom won't own up to that. I haven't met him, but I guess that's all right."

"When I got my first signing bonus, I bought her a house in a Houston suburb. Not that I can ever repay her for everything she did for me. She worked two jobs to keep us afloat and I intend to make sure she doesn't ever *have* to work again, unless she wants to."

"And what about Aunt Pallie?"

"Aunt Pallie kept an eye on us while Mom worked. Like I told you, she made sure we didn't get in real trouble."

"You bought her that trailer and the car, didn't you?"

Jake grinned. "Yeah, I did. I tried to buy her a house but she wouldn't move. She said she liked it where she was."

"I can certainly hear her saying that." CiCi thought about

the feisty old lady who was ready to take on the gangs to protect her chicks.

Jake was a combination of past and present elements, with all sorts of things between. Regardless of what she might have thought of him before, CiCi intended to peel back those layers to reveal the real man.

Chapter Twenty-Nine

The next Wednesday was a typical Central Texas summer day—hot, sunny and so humid you could almost wring the water out of the air. CiCi was sitting on their private bench down by the river, contemplating the recent turn of events.

Would Jake have introduced her to his oldest friends if he didn't think she was special? Probably not—no, definitely not. He had a public persona—the free-wheeling bachelor, but she knew now that was only a smoke screen for the real Jake Culpepper. Jake had a private side he rarely shared, and that was the man she loved—the guy who took care of old ladies and was loyal to lifelong friends.

And most important of all, he was nothing like her ex. Tank Tankersley was a mistake she never wanted to make again.

Camp was going to be over in a couple of days. Would she and Jake continue to see each other when they got back to Houston? This had been a terrific summer interlude, but could it become something permanent?

CiCi was still pondering all this when Jake joined her on the bench.

"A penny for your thoughts." He ran a finger up her bare arm.

"I was thinking about our trip."

"That's good." He flashed her a cocky grin that almost took her breath away. "So what do you think of this?" Jake slid her onto his lap and went for a slow, sensual, oh my God kiss.

"Hmm." CiCi's cognitive powers had taken a hike and that was about as much as she could manage in terms of a response. As much as she hated to admit it, she was so much in love with him it was sometimes hard to breathe.

Jake's hand trailed up under her tank top, edging toward her lacy Victoria's Secret bra. Keep going, big boy!

"Ms. Hurst, Ms. Hurst." CiCi's walkie-talkie squawked to life. "Your parents called and said they'll be here in thirty minutes."

She punched the on button and answered. "Thanks for the heads-up."

Darn it! She slipped off Jake's lap. "Rain check?"

"You'd better believe it."

EXACTLY A HALF AN HOUR LATER, Texas Bob pulled into Camp Touchdown.

"Son, have you seen this?" The man was waving a copy of the *Texas Tattler*. Why was he babbling on about some newspaper?

"CiCi." Marianne Hurst quickly joined her husband near the lodge and hugged her daughter. The woman might be a size two, but she was a larger-than-life presence. A trickle of tears accompanied her hug.

What was going on?

"You should buy waterproof." CiCi touched her mom's cheek.

"What?" Marianne seemed baffled but then she figured it out. "My mascara is running?"

"Yep."

"Winston, get over here and console our daughter. I have to go inside." She made a beeline for the ladies' room.

"What's happening?" Jake asked.

CiCi shrugged. "Beats me."

"Baby girl." Texas Bob enfolding his daughter in a smothering embrace.

"Daddy, I'm fine." CiCi's protest was muffled by Texas Bob's girth.

"Sir, Mr. Hurst," Jake said. "I think you're suffocating her." If CiCi had been any shorter, she probably would have passed out from lack of oxygen.

"Sorry, sweetheart. Mama and I almost freaked when Mac showed us this."

"What are you talking about?"

"This spread in the *Texas Tattler*." He opened the paper to a picture of CiCi and Jake in a telling embrace.

"It starts out with a story about the river rescue and quickly goes to hell. I might just sue them."

"Let me see that." CiCi snatched the paper out of her dad's hand and read the headline: Is the Heiress Trying to Snare the Football Hero?

The more she read the more she wanted to smack someone, preferably the idiot who wrote this tripe. According to this…this yellow journalism, she was a spoiled deb without a brain who was out to seduce the poor dumb jock, who also happened to be some kind of superhero.

"Bull hockey!" CiCi crumpled up the paper and was about to throw in the round file when Jake grabbed it.

"If I get my hands on that idiot with the camera I'm going to rip his head off," she said.

JAKE HADN'T SEEN this particular side of her personality. It was cute, in a tread carefully kind of way. He couldn't believe what he was reading. And how had they found out about the night in San Antonio?

He put his arm around CiCi's shoulders. It was as much to console her as to stake his claim. He tilted her chin up for a kiss. If the boss man didn't like it, that was too bad. Jake's first hint of doubt came when he realized she was as stiff as a marble statue.

"So that's the way it is." Texas Bob whipped his Stetson off his head and slapped it on his leg.

"Yes, sir, it is," Jake said. He didn't much care what Texas Bob thought. Being a free agent wouldn't be all that terrible. And if he was relegated to catching passes in the Arctic, so be it.

CiCi didn't say a word, and her deer-in-the-headlights look didn't do much to bolster Jake's confidence. What if he'd risked his career and she didn't give a flying fig about him?

He didn't have a chance to ponder the question before Marianne Hurst returned.

"Mama," Texas Bob said, "it seems our little girl and Mr. Culpepper are an item."

"Oh. Why don't we go inside and discuss what we should do next." Marianne addressed her husband, but Jake knew Texas Bob wasn't her primary audience.

"Come along, Mr. Culpepper, this involves you."

Chapter Thirty

Marianne Hurst's expression didn't bode well for the upcoming conversation, but Jake took it like a man and followed the family to CiCi's room. It would help if CiCi would give him a sign—a nod or a wink, something to confirm they were a team.

CiCi plopped on the couch with her parents bracketing her, leaving Jake the rocking chair.

"So how did the paparazzi get these pictures?" Texas Bob put his hands on his knees.

"It had to have been the guy we ran off. He obviously came back." CiCi shook her head. Jake was glad the pictures were as innocent as they were. It could have been so much worse.

"Don't worry, we'll weather the storm," Marianne said with a decided nod. "You're consenting adults and what you decide to do is your business."

Jake would bet his bottom dollar there wasn't a person in the Hursts' social circle stupid enough to mention the article.

She turned to Jake. "I'm sure you'll be glad to get back to Houston, won't you?"

"Yes, ma'am." He hesitated for a moment, but decided to clarify the situation. "Your daughter and I have a very special relationship and I intend to keep seeing her when we get home." He waited for CiCi to back him up, but she didn't say a word. Okay, she'd been under a lot of stress. For now, he'd give her a pass.

"I presume CiCi told you about her marriage."

"Yes, ma'am." He was *not* going to let a petite mom intimidate him. "I'm not Tankersley and I do *not* plan to hurt your daughter. You have my word on it."

Marianne was about to say something when CiCi interrupted. "Hey, I'm right here. Stop talking about me like I'm invisible."

"Oh, honey. You're certainly not invisible." Marianne raised her hand in contrition. "I'll be quiet."

CiCi COULDN'T BELIEVE she was behaving like such a brat. First she'd pitched a hissy fit, and then she'd totally clammed up. When Jake told her folks they were an item, she hadn't said a word. And when Jake announced he wanted to date her when they got back to Houston, she still couldn't speak. Obviously most of her brain cells had gone MIA.

A COUPLE OF DAYS LATER the counselors were helping the kids pack and the buses were scheduled for an early morning pickup. Although the teens were griping, the college kids were all smiles. It had been a very long summer and they were ready to get back to their normal lives.

After she finished packing, CiCi and Sugar Plum wandered down to the park bench that was her and Jake's special place. She was being sappy, but sometimes a girl had a right to get mushy. As she expected, Jake was there.

"I thought you might come," he said, patting the bench.

She sat next to him and laid her head on his shoulder. "This is the first place you kissed me."

"I remember." He was wearing that cocky grin again. "I plan to do it again." And he did.

Kissing Jake was the most natural thing in the world. At

times it was so hot CiCi was afraid her head would explode. Occasionally it was soft, sweet and more comforting than sensual. This kiss, however, was far removed from anything before.

It was cerebral consummation.

It was bliss.

It was…whew!

Jake was the first to pull away. He rested his forehead on hers. "I want to take you out on a real date when we get home."

That was exactly what she wanted to hear. CiCi's greatest fear—and one she hadn't expressed, even to herself—was that he'd relegate what they had to summer fling. No matter how enamored he thought he was now, with all the names in his Rolodex, there was always the chance he'd go back to his old life and she'd never hear from him again.

"You mean, like go out to dinner, museums and the opera?"

Jake laughed. "Dinner's good, but not the opera. I'm afraid that's a no-go."

CiCi threw her arms around his neck. "I don't like it, either."

"Was that a pop quiz?"

"Yep."

"And I passed?" He was acting like a kid expecting a blue ribbon.

"With flying colors."

Sugar Plum put her head in Jake's lap. She wanted some attention, too.

"I suppose we need to go to bed."

Jake finished her sentence. "Together?"

"Not tonight." She gave him a playful punch. "We have to get up early to get the little darlings on the buses. But soon."

"Promise?" He shot her that expectant grin again.

"Absolutely," she said, diving in for a delectable last taste.

Sugar Plum wanted to get in on the action so she nudged her head between them, and she was a hundred and twenty-five pounds, so they had to let her.

"I'm sorry I freaked out about the tabloid newspaper." She shook her head. "I don't know why it upset me so much. The only thing I can say is I thought it would scare you off."

"Aw, sweetheart, I realize I'm fair game. I just ignore that crap. But I hate that it upset you."

Chapter Thirty-One

Three whole days had passed since they'd returned to Houston and CiCi hadn't heard a word from Jake. Daddy said he was busy with the team, but so what? They couldn't be practicing twenty-four hours a day. If he wouldn't call her, she'd take matters into her own hands.

However, getting in touch with Jake wasn't quite as easy as she thought. He wasn't home and he wasn't answering his cell, so she left messages at both places. It wasn't until after she went to bed that CiCi heard from her missing boyfriend, lover or whatever.

"I'm sorry I haven't called," he said. "Things have been hectic. I was halfway to San Antonio when Dwayne called. Darrell had ended up in jail, again. This time it was for a bar brawl and Dwayne wanted me to pick him up. I can't believe the idiot had the gall to ask *me* for a favor."

"You didn't do it, did you?"

"Nope. But I did ream him out about the *Texas Tattler* story, and he confessed. It seems that skanky guy is a friend of his."

CiCi knew how much his family meant to him—and also how much they irritated him.

"I told Dwayne in no uncertain terms that the money well has dried up." Jake paused. "I hope he got the message.

They'd better get it together or they're going to be in a lot of trouble."

"That must've been hard, but you had to do it."

"Hey, let's talk about something more pleasant. Will you let me take you out to dinner tomorrow night? Then we can come back to my place."

His suggestion reminded CiCi that she was way too old to be living at home. It was definitely time to get a place of her own.

AFTER PICKING CiCi up the following evening, Jake whipped into his reserved spot in the underground garage. He'd probably left rubber all the way down the ramp.

"I thought we were going out to eat," CiCi teased.

"The restaurant I have in mind delivers," Jake said, hurrying CiCi to the elevator.

"Do you eat out a lot?"

He pushed the up button on the elevator. "Actually, I usually cook. It's a matter of survival. A steady diet of boxed mac and cheese got really old."

"So we're not having mac and cheese." CiCi put her arms around his neck and the conversation ceased.

The luxury condo with its expansive view of the city lights was Jake's reward for years of hard work.

"This is my home, sweet home." He ushered CiCi into the professionally decorated room featuring floor-to-ceiling windows, and steered her over to the glass.

"What do you think of the view?"

The city lay at CiCi's feet all gussied up like a Las Vegas showgirl. It was beautiful, but not nearly as alluring as the man standing next to her.

"I'm afraid of heights but I love checking out the view from tall buildings."

"Me, too, to both." Jake pulled her into his arms. "So, should I order dinner or would you prefer a little appetizer?"

The glint in his eye was impossible to miss. And sure enough, he didn't give her a chance to answer before delving into a no-holds-barred kiss.

If she could have, CiCi would have burrowed into his skin. When he lifted her blouse and spread his fingers over her bare stomach, she reminded herself to breathe. Breathing was almost impossible when Jake lightly brushed his fingers over her nipple. Then he replaced his fingers with his mouth, suckling her through the fabric of her lacy bra.

Somehow that was almost more erotic than if he'd removed her bra. And when he went for a series of warm kisses and gentle nibbles on her neck, she was a goner.

CiCi realized that sex had never been like this with Tank. That cretin was more of a thirty-second kind of guy, while Jake was a man who took his time. And as they say in country music—that ain't too shabby.

Much later Jake was spooning her, his hand on her breast and his breath tickling her neck.

"Can you spend the night?" He kissed the side of her neck before licking her ear. "I'll fix you breakfast. I make a mean omelet." Jake sweetened the deal by a flurry of kisses down the ridge of her spine.

Oh my God, oh my God, oh my God. Breakfast? Was he kidding? She was ready to eat him up and he was discussing eggs?

"What's on the menu?" CiCi couldn't resist the double entendre.

"We'll see," he said, turning her face to capture her lips in another deep kiss.

THE NEXT MORNING when Jake walked her to her parents' front door, CiCi felt like a naughty teen. Soon, very soon, she'd have her own place and Jake would be welcome anytime. His chrome-and-glass bachelor pad was beautiful, but it didn't feel very homey. And try as she might, CiCi couldn't shake the thought that he'd entertained other women there.

"Would you like to come in for a cup of coffee?"

Jake paused before answering. "Can I pass without making you mad?"

"You don't want to run into Daddy, do you?"

"No," he admitted sheepishly. "That's not at the top of my list."

"Oh, really." She ran her hands up under his Road Runner T-shirt, disregarding the fact they were standing on the front porch in the broad daylight. CiCi reveled in what she could do to him. And the things he could do to her—

He pulled her hands out of his shirt, manacling her wrists at his chest. "I have to attend a formal dinner tomorrow night. Will you go with me? I totally forgot about it or I would have asked earlier."

"Formal?" Although she'd been to more than her share of fund-raisers and dinners, and possessed a closet full of cocktail dresses and ball gowns, that was her personal idea of hell.

"Will you mind if I say no? I'm not sure I'm up to anything formal quite yet." What she didn't want to face was anyone with a camera or a microphone.

Chapter Thirty-Two

Bright and early Sunday morning, Mac showed up in CiCi's bedroom, clutching a copy of the *Houston Chronicle*. What now? Wasn't that the way it always happened—one day you were happy as a clam, and then someone smacked you in the face with a dead fish.

"What is it?" CiCi demanded.

Her sister could normally talk the ears off a cornstalk, but this time she just sat there, holding the paper.

"Give it to me." CiCi flipped through the pages. There was nothing incendiary on the front page. The sports section looked okay. But when she turned to the society section, there was Jake, in living color, with a redhead plastered to his arm and her lips on his cheek.

"That...that...donkey's butt!" She crushed the paper and made a three-pointer right into the trash can.

"I'm sure there's more to this than meets the eye. He invited you to that shindig, didn't he? He wouldn't have done that if he was planning to hook up with another woman."

"Yeah," she muttered. She trusted him, she trusted him, she trusted him. So why did this feel so yucky?

Mac obviously thought CiCi was going to faint so she pushed her head between her legs. For a tiny little thing Mac was strong—and damned mean when she wanted to be.

"What did you say? I can't understand you. Speak up."

CiCi swatted at her sister but missed. "You're smothering me!"

"Oh, okay. But you're not going anywhere near a phone until after you've cooled off." To emphasize her point Mac grabbed the cordless and stuffed it down her sweatpants.

They'd played this game throughout their adolescence, and Mac had about a fifty/fifty chance of winning.

"I know I'm overreacting. And I realize that if we want this relationship to work I have to get over my jealousy issues. I'm trying, I really am, but sometimes I have this gut reaction that I can't control." CiCi retrieved the paper and sat down on the bed to smooth it out. "Did you notice she's falling out of that dress?"

Mac grabbed the paper and studied it. "Hey, I recognize her! She tried out for the Road Runner cheerleaders. She was an okay dancer, but we thought she was skanky."

Mac handed over the phone. "I'm going to sit here and monitor your call. If you're a good girl, I'll give you some privacy. If not—" She arched a perfectly plucked eyebrow.

CiCi punched in Jake's number. One ring, two rings, three rings. If it went to four she was hanging up.

"Hey, cupcake, what are you doing up so early?" Jake sounded sleep-rumpled and sexy.

"Did I wake you?"

"Uh-huh, but it's no big deal."

She heard a rustling noise as though he was sitting up in bed.

"What's happening?"

Now that she had him on the phone, she wasn't quite sure how to begin. "Obviously you haven't seen the paper yet."

"No. Why?"

There was a pause and she could almost visualize his frown. "You're in it."

"I am?" He groaned. "Don't tell me your old man dropped my option and didn't bother to tell me."

"No, that's not it. You're on the front page of the society section."

"The society section?"

She obviously had his attention. "You're with a voluptuous young lady. In fact, it looks like she's attached to you with super glue."

"What are you talking about?" Jake was starting to sound grumpy. He'd apparently realized that her jealousy had reared its ugly head.

"If you remember, I asked *you* to that dinner. But you turned me down for no good reason that I could see, and now you're waking me up before the crack of dawn to accuse me of getting it on with some chick I don't even know? Tell you what, why don't you call me back when you're ready to play nice."

The next thing CiCi heard was a dial tone. "That didn't go well."

"I could hear him all the way over here," Mac offered. "For what it's worth, I think he's telling the truth."

"I screwed up, didn't I?"

"Yep, you sure did."

"What do I do now?"

"You get dressed, and I'm not talking a pair of skuzzy shorts and a tank top, then you go to his condo and apologize. Make it worth his while to forgive you."

"How?"

Mac gave her a classic "puleeze" look. "Tell me you didn't ask me that. Didn't you and Tank have makeup sex? Hot. Heavy. Sweaty. Makeup. Sex!"

Actually, CiCi couldn't remember ever having hot heavy sex with Tank. Their relationship hadn't been too passionate, but that wasn't something she was willing to share.

"What do I wear to a seduction?"

"Now you're talking!" Mac headed for the closet and dismissed items right and left as she made a perusal of the contents. Then she held up a pair of jeans.

"I helped you pick these out. The tags are still on them."

They were skintight and had rhinestones on the back pocket and down the sides. They'd looked okay when CiCi had tried them on, but she'd never had the guts to wear them.

"Do you really want me to show off my, um, assets like that?"

Mac shot her another withering look. "I'll bet Jake would appreciate it."

There was that. "What do I wear with them?"

"Good, you're not as obtuse as I thought." Mac rummaged through the closet and came up with a cleavage-revealing knit top in a flattering shade of red.

"Ladies in red have more fun. Get dressed and get going. You have some groveling to do." She shoved the top at CiCi. "Don't come home until you and that man of yours have kissed and made up."

"Yes, ma'am." CiCi gave her sister a mock salute.

"Go get 'em." Mac patted her on the butt and sashayed out.

JAKE COULDN'T BELIEVE CiCi had actually called him to yell about a picture in the paper. He glared at the cordless phone for several seconds before throwing it against the wall. No matter what he did, he was screwed. True, he'd had his share of women, but CiCi was special and he had no intention of running around on her.

As for the woman last night, he didn't have a clue who she was. He'd been at the entrance to the hotel waiting for his car and before he knew what was happening, she was trying to suck out his tonsils. Ironically, her friend had a camera.

Jake staggered to the kitchen in search of coffee and breakfast. He was making an omelet when his doorbell rang.

"Who is it?"

Silence.

"Uh, it's me. CiCi. I talked the doorman into letting me in."

When Jake opened the door, he almost had a coronary. CiCi had somehow turned into a red-hot mama complete with stilettos, tight jeans and cleavage.

She held up a white bakery sack and a takeout tray from Starbucks. "I came bearing gifts. May I come in?"

"Sure." Jake stepped back to allow her to enter. Who was he to turn up his nose at a peace offering, especially when she was dressed like that?

CiCi wandered toward the kitchen. She placed the sack and coffee cups on the table and then made a quick turn, bumping into his chest.

"Oops. Sorry." Her face was a cute shade of pink.

Jake deliberately stayed in her personal space. Whatever she wanted to say, she'd better do it now, because she was about to get kissed.

"I came over to apologize." She said it so quickly she was tripping over her words.

"Apologize?" Jake put his hands on her hips, pulling her into his arms. She didn't resist.

"I was jealous," she admitted, ducking her head. "I'm working on it. I'm trying to, at least."

"Oh, really?" He bracketed her face with his hands and made her look him in the eye. Conversations worked better that way. "You can trust me, I promise. I've never cheated on anyone. I think that's trashy."

CiCi responded by wrapping her arms around his neck. "I'm sorry I jumped to conclusions." She took a deep breath. "Tank destroyed my confidence."

"Yeah, I know." Jake softly kissed the side of her mouth and then he traced her lips with his tongue in a tender seduction. "Divorce sucks. I don't have any personal experience but I know a lot of people who have."

"Tank's a moron."

"That's what I've heard. Football is a small community." Jake backed her up against the wall. "Are we finished discussing the infamous William Tankersley?" He barely gave her time to answer before devouring her mouth.

From there, he quickly dispensed with her sexy duds and she wrapped her legs around him. He suckled, licked and kissed, and almost drove them both crazy before finally immersing himself in her warmth.

Making love with this woman was a heavenly combination of passion and comfort. Being with her was like coming home after a long, hard trip.

This was the thing that inspired poets, songwriters and authors to wax rhapsodically. It was love. And sure enough, it wasn't rational, logical or even comprehensible.

But it *was* damn fine.

CiCi's HEAD WAS on Jake's shoulder and she was playing with the thick dark hair on his chest. There was something incredibly sexy about just the right amount of hair on the right man.

"I want to explain why I called you." She traced a finger around his nipple.

"You're not going to get a chance to, if you keep that up." Jake imprisoned her hand under his.

CiCi laid her head on his chest, listening to the steady beat of his heart. "I want to tell you about the final straw to my marriage."

Jake stroked the back of her head. "You don't have to talk about it, really."

"No, I want to. I need you to know why I do some of the silly things I do."

"Okay, press on." He leaned back into the pillow, and let her tell her story.

"It was January and the snow in Wisconsin was driving me crazy, so I decided to go home to Houston for a week. I started feeling bad about not spending enough time with Tank so I came back a day early to surprise him. Guess who got the shock of a lifetime?" CiCi shrugged. "At least they were using the guest bedroom.

"I must have made a noise because all of a sudden they both looked at me. Tank didn't say a word but he didn't have to. We both knew it was over. When they left, I called a locksmith."

Jake ran his fingers through her hair.

"Later that night Tank tried to get in, but guess what?" CiCi giggled. "The pile of clothes and trophies I threw out on the front lawn were under inches of snow."

"Remind me not to make you mad."

"You're a smart man." She tweaked his chest hair. "I don't get mad, I get even. I've been thinking about writing a book on how to get back at your ex."

JAKE PULLED A FACE. How could anyone betray CiCi like that? She was everything he'd ever wanted in a life mate, and for him to admit that was monumental.

"Now you know why I flipped out when I saw that picture in the paper." By this time she was straddling him, making conversation very difficult.

"I've never been close enough to someone to get jealous," Jake said. He didn't think this was the time to declare his love. If he didn't have a ring, he'd at least like to be on top when he popped the question.

Chapter Thirty-Three

Training camp was a rigorous two weeks designed to get the guys ready for the NFL season. The theory was if a man could do two full-pad practices a day in a Houston summer, he could play anywhere, under any circumstances.

With the exception of the weekends, the entire team was sequestered on the University of Houston campus, so CiCi hadn't seen Jake in a couple of days. However, if she waited until evening she could get him on his cell.

Her call was about to go to voicemail when Jake answered. "What's up?"

Not a very romantic greeting. "How are things?" Now that she had him on the phone, she didn't know what to say.

"I'm too old for this stuff. I was just in the hot tub. Everything hurts." Jake ended his gripe with a groan. "What's up?"

"Daddy said you have tomorrow off. Why don't we go out for a burger or something. I have something I want to tell you."

"If you don't mind me falling asleep at the table, I'm yours." He tried, but couldn't disguise a yawn.

CiCi had decided it was time to tell him that she loved him, and didn't want to do it over the phone. "Pick me up around five?"

"You can count on it."

* * *

CiCi WAS WAITING for JAKE the next day when the doorbell rang. Her sweetie was here and her family was gone—how much better could it get? She ran to the door, jerked it open and almost fainted. Instead of Jake it was Tank!

"What do you want?"

Tank pulled a bouquet of roses from behind his back. "That isn't very friendly."

"No kidding." CiCi braced her arms on the doorjamb.

"Can I come in?" He somehow managed to look contrite. "I'd like to talk to you."

"I don't think so. If you don't mind, I'm really busy." She made the tactical error of taking her eyes off him and before she knew what had happened he'd grabbed her and planted a big wet one on her mouth. What kind of wacky-tobacky had the guy been smoking?

JAKE PULLED UP in front of the Hurst residence and carefully lowered his creaking bones from the cab of the truck. A rental car was sitting in the driveway. He was wondering who was visiting when he noticed the front door ajar.

He pushed the door the rest of the way open only to see CiCi and her ex in a world-class lip-lock. It took Jake a few seconds to sort out exactly what he was seeing, and when he did he wished he hadn't. The woman he loved was kissing Tank Tankersley. Had she been using him to make Tank jealous? Had her freak-out over that stupid picture been nothing more than a smoke screen?

Just the thought of it sent a surge of white-hot rage roaring through him. Jake took a deep breath, hoping he could get a handle on his temper.

He cleared his throat. "Why is Tankersley here?"

CiCi jerked back.

"This isn't what it looks like." She stepped away from her

ex. The big guy looked confused, but that wasn't unusual; he was more brawn than brain.

"I'm her husband. What's it to you?"

CiCi smacked Tank. "You're not my husband!"

Jake ignored her. "I guess the question should be what are *you* doing here? Don't the Packers have a training camp?"

Tank puffed up, not that he needed to—at six foot seven and three hundred and twenty-five pounds he was naturally intimidating. But that didn't matter. Jake was half a second from doing the "come on, dude, let's get with it" sign. Coach would have his butt if he had to go on the Injured Reserve list because of a fight. At the moment, Jake just didn't care.

"Not that it's any of your business, but we finished our training yesterday. I came to talk to my wife."

"Ex-wife. Ex!" CiCi exclaimed. She looked back and forth between the two men before she spoke. "Tank, it's time for you to go."

"We haven't finished our business."

CiCi put the mangled bouquet on the table. "Yes, we have. Go!" She pointed toward the door.

Tank made a show of resisting before giving in. "I'll call you later." He glared at Jake. "I'll see you on the football field, hotshot." He emphasized his pseudo-threat by slamming the door on his way out.

"Oh, Jake." CiCi moved closer and put her hand on his chest. "I'm—"

Jake stepped away. He was trying to act casual so he leaned back against the door, crossing his arms over his chest.

"Were you trying to make him jealous?"

He had to give it to her, CiCi looked genuinely confused. "Are you saying that you think that I've been trying to get Tank back? Are you *nuts?*" She poked him.

Damn, she was strong.

"You bastard! How dare you come in here and accuse me of playing you."

CiCi jabbed again. At this rate he was going to look like Swiss cheese, but he didn't dare grab her hand. That was in Chapter One of the Smart Guy's Book of Survival—don't defend yourself, not unless a deadly weapon was involved. Although that finger—

"You know what your problem is? You're an opinionated jerk. I want you out of here. Now." She pointed toward the street.

"Gladly. I suppose I was just your summer fling, huh?" It was time to retreat and regroup. Jake was barely out of the house when she slammed the door so hard the globe on the front porch light fell off and shattered.

Chapter Thirty-Four

The following week was pure agony. CiCi had thought things were bad when she split with Tank, but their marriage had been a sham. This time her heart was caved in like a post-Halloween pumpkin.

She and Jake were equally responsible for this disaster, but if they couldn't get past a simple misunderstanding, what chance did they have? Jake had jumped to an erroneous conclusion and that was a shame on him. But instead of discussing the problem like an adult, CiCi had wigged out. She didn't do that very often, but when she did, it was Lizzie Borden bad.

She had to fix the situation, but how? She'd called him dozens of times but he'd never picked up. After a couple of drive-bys of his condo, CiCi decided she was turning into a stalker. Wouldn't that make great headlines for the society page?

Nothing had worked—nothing—so until she came up with a foolproof plan, she'd simply wallow in her misery and eat chocolate. CiCi had just dug into a pint of double fudge Ben & Jerry's when Mac breezed into the kitchen. Who invited her?

"What's happening?" she asked.

"I screwed up." CiCi had somehow managed to keep the

fight off the Hurst ladies' radar screen but this was the perfect time to confide.

"What did you do?"

"I lost my cool again," she confessed.

By that time Mama had joined the party. "We want facts." She'd obviously heard CiCi's comment.

"I asked Jake out to dinner. I needed to talk to him about something, but I wouldn't say what. I was going to tell him that I loved him. But when he came by to pick me up, Tank was here."

"Tank Tankersley was here? In my house?" Mama's frown was scary.

"Yeah."

"So?" Mac asked.

"So Tank was kissing me when Jake walked in."

"Oh, boy!" Marianne exclaimed. "I can't believe that jerk came here to molest you!"

"Jake got the wrong impression. He thought I'd used him to get Tank back."

"Aw, jeeze." Although Mac expressed the sentiment, it seemed to be universal.

"He's jealous. That's a good thing." Marianne was an eternal optimist.

"He was furious. We haven't spoken since."

"Call him!" Mac should have been a camp commander.

"I did."

"Do it again."

CiCi sighed. "I did, incessantly, and then I resorted to driving by his condo." She was embarrassed to admit her stalker tactics.

"Oops." Marianne grimaced. "Don't worry. Things will work out."

CiCi didn't miss the look Mac and Mama shared. The Hurst women could be incredibly devious when they got focused.

IT TOOK Jake less than thirty seconds to realize he'd messed up and a week to try to figure out how to fix it. By now he'd procrastinated so long he was afraid it was beyond hope.

The Road Runners' first exhibition game was scheduled for next Sunday and Coach was working them mercilessly. Jake had made it through "hell camp" without injury, and in the world of professional football that was worthy of at least three cheers.

Practice was over for the day. "What are you doing for dinner?" Jake asked Cole. He was almost as tired of his own conversation as he was of his cooking.

"I have a date, sorry, guy. Why don't you call CiCi?"

Yeah, why didn't he—could it be because he was a fool?

"We're kind of on the outs."

"Too bad."

Yeah, it was too bad. To her credit, CiCi had called more than once and he'd been too chicken to respond. Or to be more specific, he wasn't sure he wanted to hear what she had to say.

Locker rooms were the same around the league—sweaty guys, trash talk, backslapping, raunchy jokes, congratulations and commiserations when team cuts were being made. Under other circumstances Jake would be in the middle of it all, but lately he hadn't been feeling very social.

He was removing his pads when Coach Carruthers strolled up to him, clipboard in hand. Crap! Things on the field had been going so well, surely he hadn't been cut. Even if he *was* on the outs with the owners baby girl.

"Hey, Culpepper. Have you been doing something I don't know about?" Coach propped one foot on the bench in front of Jake's locker.

Jake wiped his face with a towel. "I don't know what you're talking about." It was safer to just play dumb.

"The big guy wants to see you."

Jake assumed Coach meant Texas Bob, not God. But all things considered, God would probably be more sympathetic.

Jake pulled off his shirt. This wasn't the time to panic. "Do you have any idea what he wants?"

"Nope, but if I were you, I'd grab a shower and get my butt up there, ASAP." Coach was a wise man.

"I'm on my way." Jake grabbed a clean towel and a bottle of shampoo before marching off to the showers.

Twenty minutes later, he was trudging up the stairs to Texas Bob's private offices. He knew from personal experience that a royal summons was about as enjoyable as an IRS audit.

Jake took a deep breath and knocked.

"Get yourself in here."

Texas Bob's greeting blew Jake's hope for a cordial meeting.

"Yes, sir." Jake stepped into the office, expecting to see Texas Bob with his feet propped up on the desk, and he wasn't disappointed. What he hadn't anticipated was seeing Mrs. Texas Bob and Mac.

"Come in, come in, son," Texas Bob boomed. The owner's habit of speaking in capital letters had probably contributed to his business success, either through intimidation or awe. Then Jake realized what he'd heard—Texas Bob had called him *son*.

Marianne Hurst indicated a place on the couch. "Please sit down. We'd like to talk to you." She patted the cushion next to her.

"Yes, ma'am." Jake sat and propped his elbows on his knees.

"So, what can I do for you?" He pasted on a phony smile. Heck, he was a man—he could face the music, be it good, bad or indifferent.

Mac was lounging in a leather chair. She was the first to speak up. "We want to talk to you about CiCi."

Jake's patience was already stretched thin and this line of questioning wasn't helping matters. "Don't you think you should have this conversation with your sister?"

She had the grace to look embarrassed but it didn't keep her from continuing. "CiCi is impossible to live with. So, we put our heads together, and Daddy suggested we talk to you."

Texas Bob shrugged.

"Are you in love with my daughter?" Marianne asked.

The Hurst women were double-teaming him. Even Terrell Owens didn't get that much coverage.

"I don't mean to be disrespectful, but I'm not going to discuss this with you."

Marianne took his hand. "We're not trying to meddle, truly we're not. My daughter wants to fix things but she doesn't know how. She loves you."

That got his attention. "Is that what she said?" he asked Marianne.

"Well, uh…"

Okay, that was clear enough, and it wasn't the reply he wanted. "I know you mean well, but I think this meeting is going nowhere real fast. I've had a hard day, so I'll just say goodbye."

He'd stood to leave when Mac spoke again.

"She loves you," she said.

"How do you know?"

"She's been eating ice cream by the truckload. That's a clear indication of a broken heart. You guys need to get your act together."

"Isn't that the truth." Up until that point Texas Bob had kept his opinion to himself.

His wife glared at him. He put his hands up in surrender,

but ruined the effect with his next words. "That girl's driving everyone nuts."

It was perverse but Jake wanted to hear more. "I'm listening." He sat back against the sofa cushion.

"Great!" Marianne exclaimed. "Now, let's discuss our plan."

Chapter Thirty-Five

The Road Runners' first preseason game was less than a week away and CiCi hadn't made up her mind whether or not she'd attend. Her heart told her to make an appearance, no matter the consequences. Her brain said she was an idiot.

CiCi was eating a bowl of cereal in the kitchen when she heard giggles and then the patter of little feet. It was Molly and her cousin Trip.

"Aunt CiCi." Molly wrapped her arms around her aunt's waist. "Mama and Grammy have a surprise for you."

"Really, what is it?"

Molly giggled. "Silly, it wouldn't be a surprise if I told you." She grabbed CiCi's hand and tugged. Trip did the same to her other hand. CiCi didn't have any choice but to follow them to the sunroom.

At first glance it seemed as if everything was normal. Then she saw it. CiCi squinted, hoping against hope that she was hallucinating. She closed her eyes, shook her head and willed it all away.

Nope, it was still there on the couch. CiCi shot her relatives the evil eye. "What is Tex the Chicken doing here?" CiCi plopped into one of the easy chairs.

"Baby doll," Daddy began but was quickly overpowered by the cacophony of female voices, including Mac, Mia and Mama.

"Girls, let me explain it." Mama was obviously the chief conspirator.

At first it looked like there was someone in the mascot suit, but then CiCi realized the red-crested chicken head was listing at half-mast.

"Daddy needs a favor," Mac said.

CiCi glanced at her father. "If *Daddy* needs a favor, why doesn't *Daddy* ask me?"

Her disdain obviously wasn't lost on Texas Bob. "It's like this. Our newest mascot's taken a hike and we need a stand-in for the first preseason game." He rolled his shoulders. "I have the front office looking for a permanent replacement, but for the time being..."

Benedict Arnold would fit right in with this family. "After everything that's happened, what makes you think I'd do this, even for just one game?"

Texas Bob put his chin in his hands. "We're in a bind. Mac is too short and your mom is too, uh, mature." As an afterthought, he gave his wife a wink. "Isn't that right, snookums?"

"Don't 'snookums' me," Marianne retorted before turning her attention to her youngest daughter. "Seriously, we don't have anyone else who can do this, and what would a game be without Tex the Road Runner?"

Mama had a point. "Oh, okay. But keep in mind this is temporary. One game only." CiCi's inner voice was screaming like a banshee for her not to do this.

Too bad she couldn't hear it because of the racket her heart was making. Her family was obviously up to something, she just couldn't tell what. Unfortunately, she knew this "little favor" was going to turn out to be a whole lot bigger.

JAKE HAD a bottle of beer in one hand and a bag of chips in the other. He was dead tired and looking for some mindless entertainment, but the phone rang. He checked the caller ID and discovered it was Texas Bob's cell.

"Hello, sir," Jake answered.

"It's a go. CiCi will be the mascot on Sunday. The ball is in your court now, son."

That was what Jake wanted to hear, so why was his gut twisted like a pretzel? Perhaps he wasn't looking forward to making a fool of himself on national TV. "Got it. I'll take care of everything. Thanks."

After Jake clicked off, he flopped on the couch. *Why* had he agreed to this insanity? It wasn't too late to back out, but did he want to? He desperately needed CiCi in his life.

Jake stabbed a series of numbers into his cordless phone. No time like the present to call in a few favors. He hoped like heck he wasn't making the biggest mistake of his life.

"Whatcha need?" The voice on the other end was a southern drawl familiar to any fan of NFL Sunday.

"Didn't your mama teach you any manners?" Jake quipped.

"Yep, she sure did, but I've got caller ID and I know it's you. So I don't have to be nice." The man tempered his insult with a chuckle.

After a few more good-natured jabs, Jake got down to business. "Hey, Fullbright. I've got myself a big problem and I need some help."

Jake's explanation was met with silence. That wasn't encouraging. "So what do you think?"

"Dude, you gotta be jokin'. Right?"

"Nope, I'm dead serious." Oh, man, this had the earmarks of being a huge goat rope but he was determined to succeed. And if the broadcast network didn't agree to help, he was going to have to come up with Plan B.

Fullbright reacted with a huge belly laugh. "I can't wait to see this. What do you need me to do?"

"Grease the skids for me. Convince the network to play along."

"Who am I to get in the way of true love? I'll see what I can do. Call you later."

That was as much as Jake could ask for. "Great. Thanks, I owe you."

"You sure do, and don't think I won't collect."

"That wouldn't enter my mind. I'll buy you dinner the next time you're in Houston."

"I'm gonna soak you for the biggest steak in town."

"It's yours."

Jake hung up and put his head in his hands. If they pulled this off it would be a miracle.

Chapter Thirty-Six

Sunday finally rolled around. The game was in full swing and Jake was sweating bullets. He wasn't intimidated by the massive linemen who were trying to kill him. He wasn't in awe of the coaches, or the fans or even Texas Bob. He was, however, terrified of a woman in a chicken suit.

The Road Runner defense was on the field. It was a fourth down and less than a foot for the other team. Under ordinary circumstances he'd be at the yard marker, yelling encouragement. Not this time.

Cole popped him on the arm. "Hey, guy, keep your mind on the game." He was the only person—other than the Hurst family and the entire broadcast staff—who knew what Jake was planning. "What can happen, other than looking like a moron on national TV?" He tempered his jibe with a huge grin.

"Screw you."

The quarterback hooted. "Not in a million years, dude, not in a million years. I sure wouldn't want to be in your shoes."

His friend had that right. Jumping into a pit of snakes sounded less scary than what he was about to do. "Thanks for your support."

The quarterback hit him on the arm again. "Good luck, man. I'm on your side." He grinned once more before turning his attention back to the game.

A roar went up and Jake realized the other team had lost the ball on downs. It was his time to hit the field. He pulled on his helmet and trotted to the huddle. Another quarter and his fate would be sealed. Was he man enough to do the job? Or would he "chicken out" and call the whole thing off?

"CULPEPPER, NEXT TIME I throw you a ball, you catch it, ya hear? You're not up to snuff here." Cole's patience was about to run out.

"No kiddin'. Ya better keep your mind on the game or the coach is gonna have you out here running wind sprints." That pearl of wisdom came from a 300-pound linebacker. Irritating the offensive line was never a good idea, not unless Jake was hankering for a torn ACL.

On the next pass play, he tried for a diving catch and missed. It was third down when Cole threw a perfect spiral to another receiver, who sprinted toward the goal line.

Touchdown! A point after touchdown kick and the score was seven/zip. Jake had to get his head back in the game, at least until the halftime. The next series of downs produced an amazing run into the end zone for the opposing team. It was seven/seven and Jake hadn't done a darned thing to help the team.

"The next one's gonna be yours. Don't mess it up," Cole said.

Don't mess it up, don't mess it up. If the cameras hadn't been on them, Jake would have shot his old buddy the one-fingered salute of friendship.

The next offensive play was a pass to Jake that gave them a first down. Three series later and they were in the end zone for another touchdown. When the buzzer sounded, the score was fourteen to seven.

And it was showtime!

* * *

THE STUPID CHICKEN SUIT was stifling. Why had CiCi agreed to this lunacy? A smart girl would be up in the luxury box enjoying a frozen margarita, not down on the sidelines in a smelly mascot costume.

The crowd roared. What had she missed? She checked the peephole and saw that Jake's teammates were slapping him on the back. CiCi jumped up and down flapping her wings. Of course, her enthusiasm had nothing, absolutely zilch, to do with Jake. It was her job to root for the team.

Uh-huh!

A high-school band was gathered on the sidelines for the halftime show and the dance team had formed a semi-circle around her. Before they marched on the field, she'd better get out of the way or they'd mow her down.

When the buzzer for the end of the half sounded, the Road Runner gals tightened the circle. That was CiCi's first inkling that something was up. And when the network reporter showed up, microphone in hand, she knew for sure. And that was before she spied Buster Fullbright, the national broadcast co-host, heading her way.

What in the bloody hell was going on?

SWEAT DRIPPED DOWN the back of Jake's neck and it had nothing to do with exercise. To put it succinctly, he was terrified. He signaled the cameraman and marched toward his fate.

If this harebrained scheme went south, he'd have to banish himself to the Arctic Circle. With that cheerful thought in mind, he called on every ounce of courage he could muster.

It felt like a replay of his first encounter with CiCi. Ten yards, five, three yards to the target. She was surrounded by members of the dance team. Then Cole appeared next to him—he was the ring bearer.

"I can't believe I agreed to do this," the quarterback said but his grin was the size of Texas.

Jake jabbed him, though with all the padding, it was more symbolic than effective.

"Go on," Cole prompted.

Jake grabbed the mascot's wing, hoping like heck she didn't whack him. He couldn't think of anything worse than getting decked by a six-foot chicken in front of millions of people.

Buster Fullbright gave him a sly wink.

He could do this. He could do this. He could do this. That was Jake's story and he was sticking to it.

Grabbing a handful of feathers, he dropped to one knee in front of CiCi. The camera was panning back and forth, the dance team was bouncing in place and unbelievably, the band was playing Alabama's "Will You Marry Me."

How *many* people were involved?

ALTHOUGH CICI'S FIELD OF VISION was somewhat limited by the chicken head, Buster Fullbright was hard to miss. What was he doing down on the field at halftime? It wasn't until she saw Cole that she became convinced that something strange was happening.

Then she saw Jake. He looked sort of green. When he grabbed her wing and fell to his knee, CiCi was afraid he was having a seizure.

She tried to yell "Call 911," but saying anything while wearing that stupid feather head was impossible. Everything from "go, team" to "get out of my way, you dumb cluck" came out as a garbled "humph."

The cameras were rolling, Fullbright was grinning like a court jester, Cole was holding a tiny blue shopping bag, and CiCi was ready to whip off her crested head and get on with the CPR. Then Jake held out his hand.

Was that what it looked like? This had to be a dream. Jake

Culpepper was in full pads, down on one knee and in his hand he had a ring with a diamond the size of a penny.

This was hell, pure unadulterated hell. The man she loved more than anything in the world was offering her a glimpse of heaven, and she couldn't do a thing about it because she had wings.

No fingers. Nowhere for him to put the ring. And to make matters worse, she was stuck in a stupid feathered head. Dante couldn't have come up with a more distressing scenario.

"Let me help you with that," Mac said and then CiCi noticed that her entire family was there, including Sugar Plum.

Without warning, Mac ripped off the chicken head, leaving CiCi to deal with a bad case of hat hair. She was so busy trying to tame her locks she almost missed what Jake was saying.

"Will you marry me?"

She was only vaguely aware of the band, the dancing girls, the national television camera and the crowd of thousands—make that millions. Everything was obliterated by the beat of her heart and the roar of blood gushing through her body.

Then Jake sealed the deal. He gave her one of those melt-her-bones grins and uttered the magic words: "I love you."

CiCi was flapping her wings like Foghorn Leghorn on speed, but what else could she do? She didn't have any usable appendages.

"Yes!" she screeched. The teachers from Miss Newcombe's Finishing School would be scandalized, but they'd never faced Jake Culpepper down on one knee holding out a dream. She realized that the fiasco with Tank had been nothing more than a fit of temper on both their parts.

"I love you and I trust you. How about you?" she asked with a smile.

"Oh, yeah."

"In that case, *definitely* yes." It wasn't a champagne-and-roses proposal, but it couldn't have been more perfect.

CiCi tried to kneel beside him but the darned chicken feet tripped her and they both ended up flat on the ground.

Seems turnabout was fair play. This time it was the chicken who tackled the tight end, and what could be better?

Chapter Thirty-Seven

Eight months later
Society section—Houston Chronicle—April 21

Only In Texas
Only in Texas could the society wedding of the year be held in a field of bluebonnets under the branches of an ancient live oak. But leave it to Collier Channing "CiCi" Hurst (daughter of Winston and Marianne Hurst) and Jake Culpepper, star tight end for the Road Runners, to pull it off with élan. The ceremony was held at the groom's ranch.

The bride wore a stunning Vera Wang strapless dress and carried a bouquet of bluebonnets and yellow roses. She was attended by her sisters, Mackenzie Coleman and Mia Stockton. The groomsmen included Road Runner quarterback Cole Benavides and Mr. Culpepper's cousins, Dwayne and Darrell Scruggs.

The guest list featured a glittering array of Houston society, the entire Road Runner team and the future residents of the Haven, the Culpeppers' residential facility for at-risk teens.

As an aside, the guests were advised to wear boots and to watch out for the rattlesnakes. In the spirit of the party, the bride and her party all wore hand-tooled cowboy boots.

Only in Texas!

CiCi's first wedding had been a formal affair and she was determined not to go down that path again. Her intention was good but she hadn't factored in Mama's considerable powers of persuasion. And that was why the soirée ended up a cross between a Buckingham Palace extravaganza and a Reba McEntire hoedown.

Yes to the trip to New York to purchase a Vera Wang original. No to a church wedding and a reception at the country club.

CiCi had her heart set on getting married in a field of wildflowers at Jake's ranch, with a huge barbecue to follow. If Mama wanted that catered, so be it—just as long as the dudes doing the cooking wore jeans and Tony Lamas.

And speaking of boots, Daddy had a friend whose brother-in-law was known as the Van Gogh of boot making. The pair he created for CiCi was a masterpiece. Everyone in the bridal party—Mama included—was fitted for boots. This was Texas in the spring and smart folks didn't tromp around a field during rattlesnake season without protective footwear.

The big day was finally here, and it was glorious. The sun was shining, the bluebonnets and Indian paintbrush wildflowers created a vibrant sea of color, and even better, CiCi was feeling beautiful.

"You're so lucky." Mac squeezed CiCi's hand as they finished getting ready. "This is the beginning of a wonderful adventure."

"I am a lucky girl."

JAKE WAS TUGGING at his bow tie—jeans and a nice button-down shirt were more to his liking, but his mom had always dreamed of a fancy wedding for her son. Between her and Marianne Hurst, all sorts of possibilities had flown out the window—elopement to Vegas, a trip to the courthouse, a quick trip to Mexico, etc.

Even though they'd been living together at the ranch all winter, CiCi had insisted on moving into the guest room last night. She said it was bad luck to see the bride before the wedding and she wasn't taking any chances.

Jake's musings were interrupted by a tap on the door. Without waiting for a response, Cole came in, followed by Dwayne and Darrell. Cole was his usual debonair self. Dwayne and Darrell looked like waiters at an expensive restaurant. And to think, he'd sprung for tailored tuxes. He was reminded of the old saying about making a silk purse out of a sow's ear. If it had been up to Jake, they'd be sitting in the audience, but his mom had insisted they be in the wedding party. And when Mom set her mind on something—

"Are you ready?" Cole asked, adjusting Jake's tie. "There's quite a crowd out there. The whole team's already seated and they brought their wives and children."

"Have my teenage buddies shown up yet?" Over the winter, Jake and CiCi had established a foundation for at-risk adolescents. He'd set aside a hundred acres of his ranch property for a permanent group of foster homes for kids in need and called it the Haven. The first twenty residents and their surrogate parents had already been selected—Angel and Rondelle were included.

"Yep, all present and accounted for," Cole answered. "Now, let's get going. It's a good day for a wedding." He chuckled. "I've been smelling that barbecue since breakfast and it's made me mighty hungry." He rubbed his hands together.

Dwayne patted his stomach. "Me, too."

"A cold beer wouldn't hurt, either. Right?" Jake asked. He couldn't stop grinning.

"You got that one right." Cole shot Jake a grin. "You didn't ask about the bride."

That comment got Jake's attention. "What do you mean? Is there something I need to know?" He panicked momentarily, then came to his senses.

"Jerk! You're pulling my chain, aren't you?"

"Guilty as charged." Cole's expression turned sober. "I'm still not sure how your little surprise will go over. Did you clear it with Texas Bob?"

"Nope. If he doesn't like it, that's too bad."

Cole and Dwayne shared a look. "It's not my neck," the quarterback said. "I hear the music and that's our cue."

Texas Bob had hired an up-and-coming Texas country music band to play at both the wedding and the reception. Nothing was too good, or too expensive, for his baby girl.

Jake was having second thoughts about his secret grooms-man. The plan had been hatched over a six-pack of beer. It had seemed like a great idea then, but now he wasn't quite sure. But it was too late to call it off. Please God, CiCi would find it funny.

"Okay." Jake straightened his tie for the last time. "I'm ready. We need to get you hitched, too," Jake told his friend.

"You'll have to check with Mac on that one." Cole and Mac had an on-again, off-again relationship. Jake knew his friend was smitten.

"Let's go," he said.

CiCi CLUTCHED her dad's arm as the wedding party formed for the trip down the aisle. Mac gave CiCi a hug. "This is so cool. I'm incredibly happy for you."

"I'm scared to death."

"Don't be a ninny. Put a big smile on. There's a handsome groom waiting for you."

She was right. Jake was tall, broad shouldered and yummy beyond belief.

"I'm ready. Let's go, Daddy."

Texas Bob nodded and the music started.

CiCi was halfway down the aisle, acknowledging friends and enjoying the walk when she stopped stock-still. It took a few seconds to understand what she was seeing, and when her brain finally kicked in she almost died laughing.

Tex—her replacement as the Road Runner mascot—was standing beside the preacher in all his red-crested glory. Lord in heaven, life with Jake Culpepper was never going to be dull. And that was exactly the way she wanted it.

*Rancher Ramsey Westmoreland's temporary cook
is way too attractive for his liking.
Little does he know Chloe Burton came to his ranch
with another agenda entirely....*

That man across the street had to be, without a doubt, the most handsome man she'd ever seen.

Chloe Burton's pulse beat rhythmically as he stopped to talk to another man in front of a feed store. He was tall, dark and every inch of sexy—from his Stetson to the well-worn leather boots on his feet. And from the way his jeans and Western shirt fit his broad muscular shoulders, it was quite obvious he had everything it took to separate the men from the boys. The *combination* was enough to corrupt any woman's mind and had her weakening even from a distance. Her body felt flushed. It was hot. Unsettled.

Over the past year the only male who had gotten her time and attention had been the e-mail. That was simply pathetic, especially since now she was practically drooling simply at the sight of a man. Even his stance—both hands in his jeans pockets, legs braced apart, was a pose she would carry to her dreams.

And he was smiling, evidently enjoying the conversation being exchanged. He had dimples, incredibly sexy dimples in not one but both cheeks.

"What are you staring at, Clo?"

Chloe nearly jumped. She'd forgotten she had a lunch date. She glanced over the table at her best friend from college, Lucia Conyers.

"Take a look at that man across the street in the blue shirt, Lucia. Will he not be perfect for Denver's first issue of *Simply*

Irresistible or what?" Chloe asked with so much excitement she almost couldn't stand it.

She was the owner of *Simply Irresistible,* a magazine for today's up-and-coming woman. Their once-a-year Irresistible Man cover, which highlighted a man the magazine felt deserved the honor, had increased sales enough for Chloe to open a Denver office.

When Lucia didn't say anything but kept staring, Chloe's smile widened. "Well?"

Lucia glanced across the booth at her. "Since you asked, I'll tell you what I see. One of the Westmorelands—Ramsey Westmoreland. And yes, he'd be perfect for the cover, but he won't do it."

Chloe raised a brow. "He'd get paid for his services, of course."

Lucia laughed and shook her head. "Getting paid won't be the issue, Clo—Ramsey is one of the wealthiest sheep ranchers in this part of Colorado. But everyone knows what a private person he is. Trust me—he won't do it."

Chloe couldn't help but smile. The man was the epitome of what she was looking for in a magazine cover and she was determined that whatever it took, he would be it.

"Umm, I don't like that look on your face, Chloe. I've seen it before and know exactly what it means."

She watched as Ramsey Westmoreland entered the store with a swagger that made her almost breathless. She *would* be seeing him again.

Look for Silhouette Desire's
HOT WESTMORELAND NIGHTS
by Brenda Jackson,
available March 9 wherever books are sold.

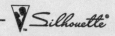

SPECIAL EDITION

FROM *USA TODAY* BESTSELLING AUTHOR

CHRISTINE RIMMER

A BRIDE FOR JERICHO BRAVO

Marnie Jones had long ago buried her wild-child impulses and opted to be "safe," romantically speaking. But one look at born rebel Jericho Bravo and she began to wonder if her thrill-seeking side was about to be revived. Because if ever there was a man worth taking a chance on, there he was, right within her grasp....

Available in March
wherever books are sold.

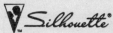

REQUEST YOUR FREE BOOKS!
2 FREE NOVELS PLUS 2 FREE GIFTS!

HARLEQUIN®

American Romance®

Love, Home & Happiness!

YES! Please send me 2 FREE Harlequin® American Romance® novels and my 2 FREE gifts (gifts are worth about $10). After receiving them, if I don't wish to receive any more books, I can return the shipping statement marked "cancel." If I don't cancel, I will receive 4 brand-new novels every month and be billed just $4.24 per book in the U.S. or $4.99 per book in Canada. That's a saving of close to 15% off the cover price! It's quite a bargain! Shipping and handling is just 50¢ per book in the U.S. and 75¢ per book in Canada.* I understand that accepting the 2 free books and gifts places me under no obligation to buy anything. I can always return a shipment and cancel at any time. Even if I never buy another book from Harlequin, the two free books and gifts are mine to keep forever.

154 HDN E4CC   354 HDN E4CN

Name   (PLEASE PRINT)

Address   Apt. #

City   State/Prov.   Zip/Postal Code

Signature (if under 18, a parent or guardian must sign)

Mail to the **Harlequin Reader Service:**
IN U.S.A.: P.O. Box 1867, Buffalo, NY 14240-1867
IN CANADA: P.O. Box 609, Fort Erie, Ontario L2A 5X3

Not valid for current subscribers to Harlequin® American Romance® books.

Want to try two free books from another line?
Call **1-800-873-8635** or visit www.morefreebooks.com.

* Terms and prices subject to change without notice. Prices do not include applicable taxes. N.Y. residents add applicable sales tax. Canadian residents will be charged applicable provincial taxes and GST. Offer not valid in Quebec. This offer is limited to one order per household. All orders subject to approval. Credit or debit balances in a customer's account(s) may be offset by any other outstanding balance owed by or to the customer. Please allow 4 to 6 weeks for delivery. Offer available while quantities last.

Your Privacy: Harlequin is committed to protecting your privacy. Our Privacy Policy is available online at www.eHarlequin.com or upon request from the Reader Service. From time to time we make our lists of customers available to reputable third parties who may have a product or service of interest to you. If you would prefer we not share your name and address, please check here. ☐

Help us get it right—We strive for accurate, respectful and relevant communications. To clarify or modify your communication preferences, visit us at www.ReaderService.com/consumerchoice.

HAR10

Silhouette *Desire*

THE WESTMORELANDS

NEW YORK TIMES
bestselling author

BRENDA JACKSON

HOT WESTMORELAND NIGHTS

Ramsey Westmoreland knew better than to lust after the hired help. But Chloe, the new cook, was just so delectable. Though their affair was growing steamier, Chloe's motives became suspicious. And when he learned Chloe was carrying his child this Westmoreland Rancher had to choose between pride or duty.

Available March 2010 wherever books are sold.

Always Powerful, Passionate and Provocative.